I0748227

More Aster(ix) Anthologies

Longing
Fall 2024

Bending
Spring 2024

10th Anniversary Issue, Part II: Fiction & Interviews
Fall/Winter 2023

10th Anniversary Issue: Part I - Poetry & Nonfiction
April 2023

The Tarot Issue
December 2022

Mothers Unearthed
September 2022

Winter Fiction
December 2021

Best of Hot Metal Bridge
April 2021

The Ferrante Project
October 2020

The Poetry Issue
Winter 2020

and more!

available to order in-print online

don't forget to visit
asterixjournal.com
for more content and information

Aster(ix) Journal
www.asterixjournal.com

Editor-in-Chief/Founder
Angie Cruz

Publisher/Founder
Adriana E. Ramíre

Senior Editors
Tanya Shirazi Galvez
Amanda Tien

Managing Editor
David Lo

Contributing Editors
for *Debut Fiction*
Cinthya Bolaños Zamora
Lila Bonow
Aya Burton
Tyler Henderson
Sofia Garner
Sandra Lee
Lissette Norman

Aster(ix) Contributing Editors
Rosa Alcalá, Arielle Greenberg, Yona Harvey, Daisy Hernández, J. A. Howard, Sheila Maldonado, Dawn Lundy Martin, Oindrila Mukherjee, Idra Novey, Emily Raboteau, Nelly Rosario, Zohra Saed, Sun Yung Shin, Jenelle Troxell, Chika Unigwe, Marta Lucía Vargas, Autumn Womack, and in loving memory, Elleni Centime Zeleke

Advisory Editors
Ari Ariel, Armando Garcia, Amy Sara Carroll, Norma Cantú, Xochi Candalaria, Jennifer Clement, Edwidge Danticat, Cristina García, Stephanie Elizondo Griest, Andrea Thome, Helena Maria Viramontes

Aster(ix) print issues are published twice a year with additional content online.

Aster(ix) is funded in part by the Dietrich School of Arts and Sciences and the Department of English at University of Pittsburgh.

Aster(ix) Journal

presents

Debut Fiction

Edited by
Cleyvis Natera

April 2025

BLUE SKETCH PRESS | PITTSBURGH

Published via Blue Sketch Press, Pittsburgh.
www.bluesketchpress.com

Debut Fiction.
An Aster(ix) Anthology / Aster(ix) Journal
Edited by Cleyvis Natera—1st ed.

ISBN (print)   978-1-942547-24-2 (trade paperback)

Cover art by Scherezade García.
Cover Design by Little Owl Creative and Amanda Tien.

First Edition: April 2025

Printed in the United States of America
9 8 7 6 5 4 3 2 1

Contents

* * *

Featuring debut short stories and debut novel excerpts:

He told a story about a group of children who were stolen by soldiers during a military raid and left at an orphanage in the capital. The children grew up believing they were orphans.

He had his comb in his shirt pocket, as he always did. He could no longer comb his hair, but he kept patting his chest to make sure it was still there.

We moved and spun and jutted out our legs and arms, grabbing the ball, pausing. Papa says basketball is like Jazz—uncontrollable, beautiful in the rhythm, speed, and the coming together.

You, who always found the spirituality and attachment to mysticism from back home, primitive, and provincial. Look at you, turning the statue upside down, wrapping its eyes, binding it with strings. You catch yourself and think: I'm losing my fucking mind.

* * *

LETTER FROM THE EDITOR

Cleyvis Natera

My fascination with debut fiction took hold during the early months of my graduate study in creative writing. Though some of my professors insisted on pointing us deep into the canon, to a giant's later work as the map that would aid (and guide) us in discovering that brilliance within our own work, it was the late Paule Marshall who introduced the wisdom held in the wild possibility inherent in a debut writers' first work. Writers like Edwidge Danticat, Junot Díaz, and Jamaica Kincaid—people whose work burned with a distinction that glistened with beauty and pain, por supuesto, but also, irreverence, humor, joy, surprise. *These are the ones whose break from convention,* she would say in her stern and very serious tone, *stems from their loyalty to their unique voice, to their unwavering fixation in telling a truth only they know based on their own lived experience.* It was in her craft of fiction class that it first occurred to me that boldness and ambition could be nestled in the unexpected curve of a sentence. But that it also ought to reflect something that hasn't yet been said in a centuries-old conversation writers have been having with readers, with each other. She assured us that much remained unsaid and she fixed her gaze on me. And looking around that classroom in the west village, I understood the invitation, an obligation and a charge.

There is no way I could have known that my own journey to debuting as a published author would take nearly two decades from those days in Paule Marshall's class. *Aster(ix)* is the first journal that published my fiction in print, back in 2019. It would take another year to sell my debut novel, another three to have it meet the world. My editor first came across my work by reading that excerpt of *Neruda on the Park* in *Aster(ix)*. The invitation to guest edit this issue, which will be printed a few months before my second novel is published and I'm forced to leave the world of the debut writer behind forever, is profoundly meaningful to me. Yet, also, bittersweet. Over the last twenty years, my fascination with debut fiction has fastened into devotion: the most daring and exciting work happening in fiction today is found in the pages of new writers.

The fifteen writers selected for this issue are remarkable in such unique ways. Yet, there are throughlines. A concern many of these stories share is a central fixation with loss: for the language, country and family Nina may never know in Frankie Ochoa's mesmerizing "Citizen of Memory," for the loved ones who have left us in the devastating "Opa's Wake" by Cristina Herrera Mezgravis and the soul-stirring "I Find My Dead Father at the Local Supermarket" by Pilar García Guzmán. The complexities of friendship and families—by blood and those made by circumstances— are illuminated to terrific effect in Sabrina Shie's "Swimmers," as well as Kleaver Cruz's "Un Buen Tiempo," and Alba Delia Hernández's "Who We Walk With." I laughed aloud, delighted at the spiritual intervention required to bring two lovers together in Leo Martinez's polyphonic "Say A Lil Prayer." I was inspired into deep contemplation by the intertextual musings in Anna Kreienberg's "Schlegel's Fragments." I was moved by the beauty of the poetic lyricism in Nicole Counts' "Collarbone & Shoulder." "The Attic is Missing" by Aimee R. Cervenka, startled me the way only good fiction can, which is to say, it woke me up. Naima Ramos-Chapman's "Spell it Different, Take Up Space" was fresh and exciting. Ellen Hagan's "Bored of Education" got me all the way riled up. Dionne Ford's "Real Americans" has haunted me since I read it; I keep thinking about those two women, that flag. And, most seriously, an issue wouldn't be me if it didn't make the reader horny—thank you, Paloma Nieto, for your deep exploration of loneliness in "San Antonio de Padua, Patron Saint of Single Ladies." In the closing story, Zabe Bent's "Living in America," I was heartbroken when a child of immigrants decides he no longer wants to visit his parents' home country—and wondered what kinds of futures we all may make for ourselves.

Because of the amount of rejection I've faced in my life as a writer, I also want to take a moment to speak to the hundreds of writers whose submissions were not selected. Stay on it. Don't give up. Reading your work, collectively, has cemented my devotion for emerging writers and debut writers into awe even as I prepare to leave your midst. Take it from me. Even if it doesn't seem like it, you are incredibly close.

I hope you each love this issue as much I loved selecting each individual story and novel excerpt. It was as if Paule Marshall leaned over my shoulder from that other place, as I landed on each choice. Persistent, proud. *A unique voice,* she said, *an unwavering fixation with telling the truth.*

Citizen Of Memory

Frankie Ochoa

I met Violeta when I was twenty, on my first trip back to El Salvador in 2002. I flew overnight from San Francisco to Comalapa and spent the whole trip staring out the window into the darkness, waiting to catch a glimpse of the country of my birth, a country I hadn't seen since infancy. The professors that I work for had connected me with an organization, the Memory Seekers, Los Buscadores de la Memoria. Our department had just begun partnering with them to process DNA collected from adoptees like me, and from the families whose children disappeared during the civil war. Though at the time I was unaware, the department had already tapped me to be their adoptee ambassador, their mascot.

A few hours in, we hit turbulence, and the plane trembled and dropped altitude, a split second of free-fall. The cabin filled with whispers, the woman beside me made the sign of the cross, and I curled my knees into my chest and held myself tightly. I remembered anxiously that one of the professor's had said TACA, the airline I had booked, was known as the *Take-A-Coffin Along* airline. There had been a crash or two, but not to worry, he'd ridden on TACA plenty of times. He'd said it as though this would impress me or impress upon me that he'd been brave enough to leave the comforts of the first world and fly headfirst into danger.

When I told my mothers what he'd said, the color left their faces. Stevie laughed it off and told yet another story about backpacking through London when she'd been my age. Denise tucked photocopies of my passport into every piece of clothing I packed, like that magic paper was an amulet against death. But I wasn't afraid of injury or traveling alone. I feared arriving to a home that I'd forgotten or, worse, had forgotten me.

Just as we began our descent, the sun rose. I'd never seen a place brimming with so much green. The plane glided past a beach and turned around over the ocean to land smoothly on the runway. Immediately when I exited the plane, I noticed the density of the air: it felt heavier, the heat prickled. My senses were wide awake, even after a sleepless night. I wanted to pour every detail into my memory. At customs, the agent spoke to me in Spanish, evidence that I blended in. I tried not to let his confused look, when I answered him haltingly, disturb this illusion.

My grandmother's housekeeper, América, had arranged for her brother to pick me up from the airport. He was standing outside the baggage claim with my name, Nina Miller, on a sign. I was disappointed he looked nothing like América—that breach in genetic inheritance. She hadn't seen her brother in over ten years, he was just a teenager when she'd left El Salvador, and she'd sent me with an enormous suitcase so full of gifts, it had to be bungee corded shut to make sure the zipper didn't burst. I presented it to him, and he gave me a goofy, delighted smile in return. I liked him immediately. He drove me to a hotel in San Salvador, the same hotel my parents stayed at when they'd adopted me nineteen years earlier.

Along the way, the brother would point and say words I would repeat back as if I had understood him. I tried to hold the words in my mind, but the letters and sounds vaporized as soon as they left my mouth. Along the road, an explosion of plants: ancient looking trees and overgrown bushes, hairy vines slithering through barbed wire fences. Vendors in brightly colored, ruffled aprons sold golden coconuts the size of bowling balls. Behind them, the shells were piled up, cut open and burning. The dense smoke curled into the car's open window.

"Aqui, creo," he said, as he turned up a manicured drive. The hotel towered over the surrounding buildings, with imposing arches and decorative roman columns. He let out a low whistle as he pulled up to the curb. I copied him, pretending to be overwhelmed with the luxury, as though I'd never seen anything so grand. The heat of embarrassment rushed through me. I prepared myself for the brother's generous smile to twist into a sneer, a "must-be-nice" look on his face, his analysis of my privilege, his recognition that I was a "fake." But the brother nodded his head with approval at the gleaming white walls. He helped me out and squeezed my hand between his, as though I was dear to him.

"Wait!" I remembered the disposable camera I'd packed. I found it in my backpack and snapped a photo. "For América," I said.

When I got to my room, I called my mothers to let them know that I'd made it. Stevie answered, "How's the hotel?"

"Fancy." I said. "I'm in room 907. Do you remember what room you were in?"

"What room were we in, Denise? Do you remember?"

I heard Denise's soft voice in the distance, "Second or third floor. It had a balcony that looked out over the pool."

I looked out my window, I was facing the front side of the building. The volcano of San Salvador towered over the skyline. "I haven't seen the pool."

"It's a nice pool," Stevie said. "Did you bring your bathing suit?"

"We saw a bomb go off from the balcony," Denise said. "The last night we were there."

"How close?" I asked.

"Too close." Stevie said.

* * *

The next morning, the Memory Seekers, Yenni and Chepe, came to get me. At the time, the two of them were the whole organization. Together they combed every corner of the country, connecting the families of the disappeared. Yenni was my age, but she seemed older. Her sparkly nail polish and the bright artisan cloth bag slung over her shoulder were so cheerful in comparison to the serious look on her face.

"Ready?" she asked, English sounded round and warm when she spoke it. She extended her hand to me. Her arms were covered in long, silky black hairs, but the hair on her head was short and frizzy. Awkwardly, I reached to shake her hand, but she laughed, took my hand in hers and walked me to the truck outside. "We are going to Nueva Esperanza." The town had many unsolved cases of missing children, and the organization was holding a Day of Memory there.

Chepe opened the truck gate. "You ride back here. It's more fun."

"How long is the ride?" I asked casually, throwing my bag onto the truck bed.

"One or two hours," Chepe said.

"Great." I climbed in beside the file boxes and DNA kits. I put my bag under my head and looked up at the morning sky, imagining my body parts scattered along a two hour stretch of road. I'd only ridden in the back of Denise's truck the few miles back and forth from the beach, packed tightly between the boogie boards and the beer cooler. The truck set off and the wind streamed around me. When my initial fear of annihilation was overwhelmed by a curiosity to see where I was, I sat up and saw many other people riding in the backs of trucks. I smiled and waved at them, and they looked at me wondering what my problem was. Chepe laughed at me as he knocked the glass and gave me a thumbs up.

Violeta greeted us as we pulled up to the town square; a lone woman with a hulking frame bossing a push-broom over the concrete. As soon as Chepe and Yenni were out of the truck, Violeta strided over, patting her small pink hands on their backs. She had baby cheeks that glowed with the sun, and small penetrating eyes. She wanted to know who I was. As Yenni explained, Violeta's eyebrows raised in curiosity. She stared straight at me, so intensely I became conscious of my own breath. She asked my age.

"Twenty," Yenni replied for me.

She pulled me under her arm and held my head against her shoulder. My body was swallowed by the largeness of her body, constricted in the muscularity of her grasp. Her hand quivered as she held me. She said something in Spanish. I looked over at Yenni for help.

"Violeta has a missing sister the same age as you. She says, whoever your family is, they haven't forgotten you." A dark flower bloomed in my chest as the sorrow in her embrace entered me. Though I'd considered it before, I sensed in my own body for the first time the quivering, terrible possibility that I had been disappeared.

People filled the town's square, standing with their arms crossed, speaking quietly. Chepe ran an extension cord from the internet cafe, past the sleeping dogs, to the little patch of shade beneath an illegible faded banner. I learned later that it had once read Bienvenido a Nueva Esperanza, and had been gifted to the town by a Swedish Delegation ten years earlier, after the Peace Accords were signed in '92. Yenni set up a table and a few chairs and I sat close beside her, so that she could translate for me. Chepe greeted the crowd. He told a story about a group of children who were stolen by soldiers during a military raid and left at an orphanage in the capital. The children grew up believing they were orphans.

"I was one of those children," Chepe said. "The first few years after the war ended, dozens of children were reunited with their families. It was as though those missing kids had only been waiting for someone to call out their names, so that they could raise up their arms and be found." He cleared his throat. "Last year, we celebrated the reunion of one lost child to his father in Morazan." The crowd nodded, knowingly. "This year we have made contact with four new children, adopted abroad. We have one with us today."

All the faces in the crowd turned toward me. I suddenly felt afraid, cracked open, like something primal oozed out of me. I'd suffered from anxiety as a child, and I felt myself sinking into that low pressure vacuum, visibly cringing, my palms dampening, my fingers turning to claws.

Some of the people in the square formed a line, maybe a dozen. Each person took a turn at the microphone, speaking the names of their missing: *Enrique, Gladys, Julian.* "The last time I saw my son, he was still afraid of the dark," a man said. Yenni translated this to me in a whisper. Violeta took her turn, her husky voice boomed through the air. "My sister Isabela disappeared. My father was carrying her in his arms. My mother found my father dead, but his arms were empty. My mother still waits for her, twenty years later. Every day she asks, where is my daughter? Where is my Isabela?"

I leaned towards Yenni and asked her, "Their DNA is in your database, right?"

She nodded. I hadn't matched anyone in their DNA Database. None of these people were looking for me. I let out a sigh of relief.

A few women walked past and stared at me. One smiled, one reached out and touched my head as though I were a sacred object.

I'd spent years tending my own wounds, the scars that formed around the edge of the unknown. I thought they were mine alone, but all these strangers shared them, too.

Yenni saw me wincing. "You give them hope," she said. Their sort of hope was no bright beacon of light, it flickered like a candle burned to the end of its wick. Their hope was full of shadow. At that time, I had just begun my search for the answer to who my birth family was, the potential overwhelmed me. These people had been searching for too long.

Violeta came and stood beside me with one hand on my shoulder and shooed away the people coming behind her like she'd claimed me. It was weirdly comforting. I felt the edges of myself tuck in so that I'd fit into whoever it was she thought she'd claimed.

When the people had finished speaking aloud the names of the disappeared, the mood shifted, blowing away like a cloud. They'd summoned the ghosts from the darkness but sent them up into the sunlight. They smiled, mingled in groups, teenagers stopped on their motorbikes to look on. Violeta invited me back to her house. Yenni told me I should go, she and Chepe had a few hours of meetings with people around town.

"She knows I don't speak Spanish, right?"

"That won't stop her," Yenni winked.

Violeta linked arms with me. We charged across the two-lane highway between the buses hurtling by, we passed the radio station, and then turned up a wide, dirt road. The hills were yellow with sun burned grass, and the sky looked oversaturated, a fluorescent blue. Men on horseback clacked by in tooled leather boots and stiff straw hats, their button-down shirts were mostly open exposing their muscled chests. I'd never seen men like that, looking like real- life cowboys. Violeta laughed, "Campesinos, bien bravos."

She pointed to a house, and I caught the soft wood of the swinging gate in my hands as we passed through. The house had several rooms that all opened onto a covered patio. A girl ran to Violeta's side. "Ella es mía," Violeta pointed to herself and smiled. Her daughter was twelve then, with long curls gelled in tight ringlets down her back. "Elena," Violeta introduced us. I held out my hand and the girl slunk against her mother, eyes to the ground, a shy smile on her lips.

I followed Violeta into one of the rooms, dark as a cave, except for a sliver of light coming through an open shutter. As my eyes adjusted, I saw a woman asleep in a hammock. Violeta leaned over her, "Mi dulcita." She pulled her mother's hands to her lips and kissed them. Violeta spoke to her mother like she was talking to a tiny child. The woman seemed immobile, her face complicated by deep wrinkles, and sunken eyes sealed tight, her lashes like stitches. I wondered how she was even alive. Her eyes fluttered, she moved her arms as if to sit up. She wanted to touch me, she reached out a hand and I hesitantly stepped nearer. Though her eyes were closed, or nearly closed, she looked at me with her face, sensing me as a newborn kitten would, head shifting ever so slightly. When my hand was in her grasp, she held it weakly. "Isabela," she said quietly. The name filled the dark corners of the room.

"No, Mama," Violeta said and kissed her again. "Hoy, no." Not today. I wasn't her daughter, but there was no one in the world I'd rather have been than Isabela. I felt myself become her, in that room, held in that fragile hand, the hand of a mother, the hand of my mother. The longing on the woman's face was so misshapen, so terrible. It was like looking into a mirror, my face inverted, the shape of what was missing, not what was there.

"I'm Nina," I offered. I could have been her daughter. I could have been Violeta's sister. What a shame that I was not.

Violeta went to the wardrobe and pulled out a photo album. She shepherded me back into the sunlight and sat me at the table on the patio—the outdoors violently bright by comparison to the little room. She flipped through the pages, describing each photo in details that I understood nothing of. As she talked, I stared off into the dirt yard which had been meticulously raked like a bonsai garden, full of skinny trees bursting with the most beautiful, flirtatious, shameless purple hibiscus flowers. Chickens strutted around the yard, their proud breasts armored in feathers of the most intricate lacework patterns. She skipped through a few pages and found a photo of herself which she pulled from the plastic sleeve and held out to me proudly. She was seventeen in the photo, the year was 1988, she stood in a forest, wearing a green shirt and a red bandana, her curly hair swept up in the wind, and a lunk of a rifle in her arms.

Yenni and Chepe and I drove back to the city late that afternoon. Violeta had not wanted me to go. She'd shown me a nearly empty room in her house that could be mine if I'd just stay, just a night, but all week if I wanted.

"Hotel," I'd said, and made what I'd hoped was a universal sign for sleeping, hands folded together under my head, eyes closed. The entire afternoon had been an extended pantomime, Violeta and her daughter trying to decipher the interpretive dance of my communication, laughing at my pronunciations. "Hotel, no," Violeta said, and dismissed the idea with her hand.

When Yenni and Chepe finally drove up in the truck to get me, Violeta was sweeping the rafters of the room to get it ready for me, "muchas arañas" she'd laughed, and that I had understood. Just the mention of spiders made a scream start to expand inside my lungs. Yenni convinced

Violeta that I had to go with them. I promised to return. I touched the arm of the old woman in her hammock and told her I'd see her again, though I never did. When I said goodbye to Violeta, she told me that we were sisters now. I assumed it was just a nice thing to say—everyone had been so welcoming to me, everyone had taken me into their hands, kept me close—but, I believed her.

* * *

On my last night in El Salvador, I went with Yenni to meet some of her friends at a bar near the office. I'd spent the two weeks taking Spanish classes and sight-seeing. I'd visited El Monumento a la Memoria y la Verdad, in Parque Cuscatlán, with twenty-five thousand names of the dead and disappeared etched into a stone wall, and teenagers making out in the grass beside it. But I'd spent most of my time in the Memory Seekers office scanning boxes of handwritten notes, photos, and all sorts of documents into a computer file, starting what would become my life's work, this database of half-memory, half-hope.

We found a table in a muraled courtyard. The crowd was mostly young people drinking beers, acting like poets. Yenni ordered food for us, fried Yucca, pupusas, and sweet beans rolled up in plantains. "Don't eat the curtido," she told me, "It will make your stomach—" she waved her hands in a circle around her belly and made a face. My gringa stomach, she meant. I resented her for that, to be made to feel like an outsider who couldn't handle a microbe. I reached a fork into the bowl of curtido, fermented cabbage, and took a bite. Yenni raised her eyebrows and laughed nervously. It was delicious.

"Brave," she said to her friends, a girl from Barcelona, and a student from University of San Salvador with an acoustic guitar across his lap and a black beret on his head. The Spaniard had a topiary of hair radiating from her underarms, and an oversized lip ring that gave her an extraordinary pout. They spoke in Spanish, occasionally glancing over at me, but I understood little and made no effort to.

A boy came and sat beside me. He had curly black hair that hung around his face and was more attractive than the boys that usually might sit beside me. He lived in Canada, but his family was from La Libertad, near the coast; they'd left El Salvador during the war. He was there for the first time in his life, taking in the *motherland*, he called it. We drank for hours, and the night air turned crisp. He fished a sweater out of his backpack, which emerged crumpled, like a piece of rotting fruit, and offered it to me. I wouldn't have, but I was cold, so I stretched the sweater over my legs. He pointed to my scars. They wrapped around my knee, crawled over my thigh, scars that had marked me before my memory began. For years I tried to get rid of the scars, with honey and baking soda, with lemon juice, onion juice, coconut oil. The scars remained, glistening, satin-smooth, hideous, but mine.

"What happened?" he asked softly. I hated that question, one more question I had no answer to. But the beer had made me as liquid as honey.

I smiled at him and said, "The war." My voice was electrified by the mystery of that dark word, *war*. Violeta had been there. I'd been there, too. He nodded with a quiet knowing, but what did either of us know? We, two children of this motherland, lost to a war we knew nothing about, but home at last.

Opa's Wake

Cristina Herrera Mezgravis

I heard Opa's last words before he died. I don't think I deserved to be the one. Ma was the one who fed him and washed his genitals and treated the sores on his back and legs. She claims to have been the closest to him of his three children. She told him her secrets, she says, and he trusted her with his. He was closer to his other grandchildren. I, on the other hand, wasn't particularly affectionate with him.

On some nights when I stayed over, while Oma was showering and Opa watched baseball, I'd climb into their bed and rest my head on his chest. I stared at his crossed feet, crooked in his white, ankle-length socks. Ma says her feet were identical to his except Opa's were more crooked because his boots were too tight when he was a kid and he couldn't buy another pair. I'd listen to the *tha, thump, tha, thump* of his heart, his ribs warm and solid under the worn fabric of his cotton shirt and wonder if I'd remember the sound after he died. Opa was the oldest person I knew.

The day of his wake, the Opa in the coffin didn't look like Opa. I'd never noticed his eyelashes being that blond. His lips were pressed tight in a grimace. Ma says the guys from the funeral home must've glued them together.

I wonder how they got his mouth to close. When we arrived at Oma's house that morning, Opa had his mouth open, as if he'd died mid-yawn. A fly darted about the room, lingering over the bed. I worried it would sneak into Opa's mouth if we weren't careful, get stuck in his throat. Tía Ilde closed his eyes, which were fixed on the wall, but she couldn't get his mouth to close. Then the neighbor tried when she came to pray the rosary. She placed one hand on his head and the other under his chin, but Opa's jaws wouldn't close.

I thought her bold. Almost rude. If Opa were alive, she wouldn't have dared place a hand on his face. Opa was an intimidating man.

When Ma and Pa went on business trips and I stayed over at Opa and Oma's place, Opa was the one to wake me up for school. Before my alarm clock went off, I'd hear his leather slippers on the tiled hallway. When the door creaked open, I'd press my eyes shut, pretending I was asleep. He'd leave the door open, and then his slippers would move away. Later, I'd hear the coins in his pant pockets and knew he'd gotten dressed. If I dared open my eyes, I'd find him in the bedroom doorway, staring at me with impatience, with fury, almost with panic. He'd hold up his wrist and hit the face of his watch—*click, click, click*. If I didn't get up, he'd fetch Oma, who'd come into my room in her nightgown. She'd take my hands and guide me to the bathroom, where she'd place them under running cold water to help wake me up.

I don't know why Opa didn't move past the bedroom doorway—why he wouldn't sit next to me in bed and take my hands like Oma did. I hated that we were fifteen, twenty minutes early to school, anyway, which left me to roam the empty hallways like a loser. Ma says Opa was like that—anxious and painstakingly punctual—because of the war. He came to Venezuela after World War II with a bomb shard stuck in his leg. He was twelve and didn't know how to speak Spanish.

"Can you imagine?" Ma asked. "Getting here and not knowing the language?"

But that was something hard for me to imagine. What I did imagine was Opa as a boy, painting lamp posts on the highway. Oma told me a German man had hired Opa and other boys who didn't know Spanish. One morning, el general Marcos Pérez Jiménez himself came to supervise their work. The sun hadn't come out when el general asked, "Are you cold, boys?" and offered them each a drink of brandy straight from his flask. I imagine Opa smiling under the lamppost, proud that el general had treated him like a man.

* * *

The morning Opa died, I woke to the sound of the light switch in the hallway and saw Ma in my bedroom door, a shadow against the light.

"Nina," she said and shuffled into my room, hugging her night robe. The mattress bent under her weight as she sat next to me.

"Opa died," she said and sniffled into my shoulder. I tried to sit up, to hold her, but Ma straightened, composing herself again.

"Let's go and help Oma?"

The thought of Oma filled me with dread. I'd seen the way she pressed her lips and looked away when Opa struggled up the stairs. She refused to leave the house, wanting to be there when the moment came. I thought she'd be relieved the moment had finally come, but when the two men with the stretcher climbed her stairs and zipped Opa up in a black leather bag, just like they'd zip up a suit, she screamed, "They're taking him! They're taking him from me!"

I clung to her waist and said, "He's no longer here, Oma. He's resting. He's finally resting now," which was code for, *You can rest, too, Oma. You can leave the house and come to my tennis matches and go to the movies with us and have coffee at our place,* but my words didn't comfort her.

When people hugged us and said that Opa was a good man, I couldn't help but wonder if they knew; if they knew he drove with a beer bottle between his thighs the day he met Oma, and that, once married, he'd invite his friends to play dominoes in their walk-in closet and Oma had to get on her hands and knees the following day and scrub the beer off the carpet and wash all the smoke-smelling clothes again. One day, tía Ilde told me, Oma found lipstick stains on Opa's shirt collar and ripped the shirt and threw the shreds out the window yelling, "I'm not washing these bitches' shirts!" He drove so drunk down the highway, tía Ilde thought the lampposts were bending and Opa had to pull over to puke.

Ma says those were different times. She doesn't like when tía Ilde tells these stories. When Pa was alive, Ma liked to ask why he couldn't be as spontaneous as Opa, who arrived from work with chocolates in his shirt pocket for his daughters, or cakes for his grandchildren's birthday parties. Who surprised Oma with a bouquet of flowers on any given day and asked her to dance after dinner in the basement while Ma and tía Ilde watched them, hidden, from the stairway. For Ma, Opa will always be the most charming man.

* * *

Ma always said that, for wakes, one dresses in black out of respect for the dead. Before Pa died, Ma went to wakes in heels, pearls, and perfume. After Pa died, she stopped going to wakes until this one. For Opa's wake, Ma wore the same blue shirt and white pants she'd put on that morning; she'd got caught up in all the paperwork and never had time to go back and change.

The guys from the funeral home dressed Opa in his blue suit. The black one wasn't ironed, so tía Ilde and Ma chose the darkest one he had. With the coffin open to his waist, we could only see his jacket, shirt and tie. We couldn't really know if he had pants on or if they put on his dress shoes—for all we know, they could've stolen them. We had to imagine his legs there, resting under the wood. For all we know, he could've been a merman.

More than once, when Opa was alive but could no longer get out of bed, Ma showed me the scar the bomb shard left on his shin. When he was a kid, Opa was helping to load bombs when one went off close by and a shard got stuck in his leg. He didn't notice it until he felt blood pool in his boot.

Opa's legs were full of freckles and sunspots. As soon as Ma pointed out the scar, I'd lose it again.

* * *

In the coffin, the only thing that still looked like Opa was his thumb. If you looked closely enough, you could still see the yellow stain he got from holding his medicine pills for too long before swallowing them.

Ma loves to say her thumb looked just like Opa's. It did look like his, especially the half-moon at the base of his nail.

* * *

Opa's car—a military green Lincoln Continental—had soft leather seats and always smelled of baked bread. He kept a red apple on his nightstand that he liked to eat before bed and a stash of dark chocolate in his night drawer. When he wasn't home from work, and we were still over for afternoon coffee, I'd sneak into his room, open the drawer and take a square. Opa never said anything. I felt it was our little secret.

* * *

The week before Opa died, we drank coffee in Oma's second floor parlor. The nurse and Ma helped Opa into his plastic chair and tucked a small towel into his shirt collar like a bib. He had his comb in his shirt pocket, as he always did. He could no longer comb his hair, but he kept patting his chest to make sure it was still there. We watched as Ma played songs for him—Julio Iglesias and Elvis Presley, the ones he liked. Ma grabbed his hands and swayed with him as if they were dancing. Sometimes, Opa remembered the songs and hummed along. But that afternoon, Opa mostly stared out at the avocado tree and picked invisible spider webs off his legs with shaky hands, lost in a world we couldn't see.

When it was time for dinner, Ma and the nurse helped him upstairs. The nurse took his left arm in the crux of her elbow, and Ma guided his right hand over the railing, pushing him from behind. She counted the steps for him, "Uno… dos…"

A few months before, Opa would've yelled, "Coño Heidi! Don't push me!" but that night he only muttered, "Ay… ay… ay…"

I stayed with Oma and tía Ilde in the parlor, looking through my phone while Ma fed him. When Ma came downstairs with the tray and the soup bowl half full, she nodded up the stairs and asked me to say goodbye.

I found Opa on his side of the bed. The lamp shone on the small kingdom of pill organizers and water glasses on his night table. The nurse sat in a plastic chair by Oma's side of the bed, where she had a better view of the TV. With pillows, they had propped Opa up so he could watch, too—though, if Opa were truly Opa, he'd be watching baseball and not a comedy show. Yet Opa didn't seem to be watching the television but the wall behind it. Whenever he got lost like that, or called us names of the no longer living, or spoke to us in a German only he understood, I wondered if he'd gone back to being that boy who'd lived through cold, remote winters. I imagined him with chubby cheeks and a beret, like I imagined children in the Second World War, walking through snowy slopes to the train station where he'd wait for his dad to come back from the front, as he did for three years until he finally came back.

I sat in the chair where Ma fed him his food. I took his coarse, freckled hand and leaned in to give him a kiss.

"Chao, Opa," I said.

He squeezed my hand.

When I leaned back, his eyes searched mine. He seemed to be looking at me—really looking.

"Ah, no," I said, "Don't be sad. Mira que I'll be back tomorrow with

Ma."

"You have to be strong, chiquita."

I sat still. I wasn't sure if he knew it was me or if he thought I was tía Ilde or Ma.

"You have to be strong," he said again and squeezed my hand tighter.

His eyes watered. My eyes watered too. I hugged him.

On the TV, the audience laughed.

"Don't worry," I said. "I'll be back tomorrow with Ma, okay?"

I gave him a kiss on his stubbled cheek. I got up and turned for the door before the nurse could see me cry. She took my place on the chair.

"My eyes itch," Opa said, reaching for her.

"Yes," the nurse said. She took the towel from his shirt collar and wiped away his tears.

Collarbone & Shoulder
(an excerpt from *Soft: A Novel For and By The Body*)

Nicole Counts

When I answered a call from an unknown number saying that Papa was in the hospital, I was at work at S.A.F.E., the public health office on campus, in the middle of ordering the condoms we sold 10 for $1 while answering anonymous emails from students that usually resulted in telling someone to go to student health ASAP. I left an email unfinished, rushing to the train station.

On my train ride to Jersey, I listen to Roy Hargrove and watch the train ride over marshes full of waving catnips, into plain, gridded farms. The horn cut through trees and homes and I watch office parks turn to row homes back to land and water. I tried to pull apart the trumpet's notes, to listen to the music, but a light vibration in my chest and neck was becoming too strong to ignore. I strained my ears trying to hear what his body and mine were saying; to hear what they needed. I closed my eyes trying to more fully enter myself. I leaned forward, bent at the waist trying to make sense of the faint twin cries I was sure were escaping the bowels of both him and I.

It wasn't until I stopped moving—from subway to train to Uber to at Mama's house to the hospital—that the muffling became clearer, that our breaths became apparent, behind my eyes, in my ears, and under my skin.

Like trees I feel our roots reach out toward each other, Papa's and mine, trying to share the burden of understanding. With each step toward him, through the hospital's doors, down the halls, in the elevators, I can feel every tendon become more and more taut, can feel mine reaching out for his, both being stretched to their limits. I get it, I think—we are at the brink, we have to pull back now or only one of us will make it.

* * *

When I get to Mama's house, the car in the driveway is covered in a light coat of dust. No one is around, the street is quiet, and despite the steady wind the trees don't move. Passing the crooked 7 above the front door, I walk quickly inside straight to Mama's bedroom, reaching for her jewelry box that houses the spare keys to my brother Nate's car. When Nate learned to drive, he got Papa's old car, a beat-up wrangler he kept so clean you'd think it was new.

I call Nate to tell him Papa broke his collarbone but his phone is off. By the time he gets out of school and track practice I'll be back home, it will be too late for him to help.

The house we grew up in was the witness to Papa's changing tides, the violent winds that came and went for as long or as little as they pleased. The evidence was in the dried vomit stains, the small cigarette burns, the bits of glass swept under the fridge, and the bottles found in every nook and cranny for months and months after he had stopped living there. No matter how much we cleaned, we always found another reminder.

The last time I visited, was when the divorce was finalized and Papa had just moved out. It took Nate, Mama, and I hours to clean the kitchen alone. We cleared the dust and rice from under cabinets and corners, scrubbed decades of grime build up from the exhaust fan, washed without abandon the grease-coated wall behind the stove. Like magic, we turned it from a speckled brown to yellow to white, again. Years of neglect covered the house, and somehow, as if being mocked, alcohol still coats everything.

"Nate *can you smell that?*" I asked. Despite the egregious use of disinfectant, the subtle wisp of cognac emanated.

"A memory of smell," Nate said, "that's all it is."

* * *

The route I take to the hospital in Trenton has me pass by the courts. Rain is coming and the air is dense with humidity, fog clouds rolled lazily across the basketball court. It' is warm for early December; steam rising off the courts in repetitive wafts, one after the other, pushed by the wind. I flick on my blinker and turn with the green light, a sign yells "WALK" but there is no one there. The court is shiny, and the wind shakes the dogwood that arches over a hoop. I watch a petal fall onto the silky court, lost in its shimmer. There is one boy there; he lifts up on his toes, taking and missing a shot. The ball bounces but not high enough. It's deflated and grey, probably as heavy and hard as the one still left in our garage.

Once, during a game of HORSE, a ball just like that one slammed into the spot between my throat and collarbone, knocking my jaw into my top teeth. Papa had yelled *you alright?*

The stunning heat of a full-grain leather ball—the ones that when weathered become coarse, their bounce deafening and thrilling, a small burst of thunder—smacking into my throat, left me speechless. Papa responded with *you're alright* before I could swallow the tears.

After that, my throat was afraid, it contracted with any extended movement like when I titled my head back to laugh or to look up at the stars. I was always afraid something or someone was going to smash my windpipe and I wouldn't see it coming.

I took a short walk around the court, failing to breathe deep. I *wanted* to keep breathing my quick, short breaths. Deep inhales threaten to open me I picked at my hands, the insides of my thumb, around my cuticles, every fingertip discolored and raw. More kids pull in, the parking lot gravel kicking up its own melody. I walk further into the park, toward the volleyball courts, my back to their shouts at each other, the balls consistent bounce. They are loud, joyous, yelling that they *gon whoop that ass, them knees is shot, can't ball like me.* My hands feel warm and when I look down, blood has sprouted. I wipe my fingers on my black sweatshirt and tuck them into my pockets. I hear one of them yell, *that nigga don't know how to stay low.* I turn and look, four boys so consumed in their trash talking. There was a day Papa and I played as the wheat and corn fields turned pink in the end-of-the-day, summer light. "Stay low," Papa yelled out, "Play on your toes." Dirt wafted up, displaced by the ball hitting the pavement. I wanted to say *I know*—I know if I play on my toes, I have more control, can manage the ball and the opponent—but didn't. Gold light fluttered across us, through sweeping green trees. I bent my knees and reached up, guiding the ball with my right hand, and shooting with the left. It went in and he rebounded for me, throwing it back. I caught it and dribbled a few times, the ball spinning left. My right leg quickly dragged behind my left, before my feet fell in line with one other, a habit I still can't get rid of. I bent and that time shot with my right, guiding with my left. When it went in, he said *Nice!* And I smiled, but this time Papa didn't pass it back, instead he started toward me.

I was too short to play real one-on-one with him. He towered over me, but I surrendered to the game. I remember ignoring my left patella thrusting down, reverberating through me. I followed his body, guarding his back. We moved and spun and jutted out our legs and arms, grabbing the ball, pausing. Papa says basketball is like Jazz—uncontrollable, beautiful in the rhythm, speed, and the coming together.

When his hand reaches up, he releases the ball into air with the flick of a wrist and the certainty of finger pads that swipe at the cloud. My hand traced the path of his; his like a single tree branch that juts out past the others, cutting through the liquid sky, saying I'm here, too.

I was so focused on our dance, on any opening to snatch the ball in its flight between pavement and hand, that I didn't see Papa raise up, I didn't see him leave the ground, his arms above his head, elbow cocked, his wrist flicks. The ball took flight without him, hitting the left corner of the backboard's rectangle. And while I watched it go in, the edges licking the net, I didn't see Papa's body come back down. His sharp, angular knees met my chest, his kneecap slamming hard enough into my collarbone, as I landed on the warm pavement. Papa fell hard besides me, both of us sprawled out in the middle of the street.

The bruise stayed for years. When I miss Papa, I press into the spot, bringing me, and him, back to the moment before we fell, when the dust danced through our movements.

I arrive at the hospital just shy of 2pm. I ride through the Polish part of Trenton with streets named after trees: Spruce, Mulberry, Pine. Main street is ripped up by tree roots; they burst through the black pavement, awakening my car, and me.

I park in the visitors parking lot and sit in Nate's car for a few seconds with eyes closed. The rain has started, slowly, and I count the drops until I reach 28 and decide it's time to get out.

When I walk into Papa's hospital room the curtains are closed, and he is asleep. My body is suddenly carbonated water, tingly and weak. My legs feel like Jell-O, too soft and unsteady, and I need to sit. I move the rolling armchair from the corner of the room to face his bed. I watch his eyes move behind his eyelids. The room smells of decades of grime and piss, rolled in dirt heated in the sun. Trenton stays on you the way the hospital's tang does, remaining no matter how much you wash.

Papa's room is larger than I expected. A nurse followed me in. She pulls the curtain back hastily, wishes me a good morning as she moves his arm gently to take his blood pressure. His hair has grown out, his curls look botched; the all-white hair stands up an inch off of his head. His clothes are balled up in a plastic bag at the bottom of the bed and his glasses are folded on the windowsill. I wonder if he can even see the trees outside his window without them on. The bare trees are sharp, they look like Papa, who looks like a stick figure laying on its side—all angles and lines, his knees jut out, Papa's elbows poke the sheets, his feet cut the covers. He wore a boxy suit to my high school graduation. He had been in disguise, dressed to hide all the parts of him that were no longer there. I knew he had lost weight since he left the house, but I didn't know how much. When I touch his shoulder, so he knows I am there, it stabs my palm. *You're sharp all over, Papa.*

The nurse pulls his blanket up to expose his feet. They look small wrapped in loose hospital socks. She wraps two cuffs around each ankle and turns on a machine that inflates the cuffs up like pool floaties. He wakes up from the sound and looks around wildly, his eyes large and concerned.

"What time is it? What time is the surgery?" he asks.

"3:18," I say.

"Samara?" he asks.

"Hi Papa, couldn't stand to be left out, eh? Had to join the hospital club?" I smile at him.

"Hi Mr. James, my name is Jess, I'll be your nurse for the afternoon shift," Nurse Jess says too loudly.

He nods and forces a smile at her. His eyes are still confused, and he looks over at me.

"Do you know when he'll be able to go up?" I ask.

"The doctor should be here soon, and then we can take you up to the surgical prep unit."

"Will I wait here?' I ask.

"You can come up with him and wait with him in the prep room before they take him back. There's a waiting room on that floor too." To Papa she says, "Mr. James, are you hungry?"

"Yes," he says, as he reaches for the menu.

The nurse laughs and says, "how many days have you been here, you know all the systems!"

"I've been here since Saturday night," he smiles, polite. He looks over at me as I try to catch my face from looking too startled. I'm not sure what I'm trying to hide, the nurse must know I just found out, I am embarrassed I didn't find out until this morning, that I didn't know he was in the hospital for three days now.

The nurse explains that the doctor hasn't been available until now. He's been on pain meds for two and a half days, stewing in the shock of his broken collarbone. I am angry, and nervous, and I pick at my hands. Last night, the drive took longer than I expected and I was anxious by the time we got home. Jon sat with me on the couch watching TV. He watched me pick at the skin around my thumbnail and he tells me to stop. I was embarrassed and too seen, so I shot Jon a dirty look, and scooted farther away from him. He sighed, and reaches for my hand, holding it until I squeezed it back. He says he loves me, and I say, *you too.* I wonder now if somehow, I knew Papa wasn't okay.

"You can eat right after surgery," she says cheerfully, pulling away the menu and putting it back on Papa's nightstand.

I stop picking and thank the nurse Jess. He closes his eyes again. My palms prickle as I make a fist, and my knees buckle. I shift; I am tender all over. I am seated, nothing has happened. I know this visceral reaction is in my head, but then I wonder if I believe "head" and "body" are really separate.

I rest my hand on my thigh. It is sore from a bruise where I ran into a coffee table. I bruise easy now, and I guess Papa breaks easy now. Papa tells me that last Saturday, he was walking to catch the last bus after an evening shift at the Amazon warehouse. The bus was running ten mins early. Papa heard it before he saw it. He tried to calculate the distance to the bus stop; it was the last bus and his only way home. He decided to run, to make up the distance. His body not what it was, his neuropathy a new hurdle he wasn't yet used to. He tripped over his feet and fell hard, his cheek to the pavement, and yelled out.

When the bus approached, it swerved to avoid running him over. Two men got off to help him on. They placed him in the front seat where he could barely sit up. Papa didn't yet know he was broken; he focused on making it home. The bus dropped him off a few feet from his apartment, and lightheaded and weak he took a seat on a bench. His phone, not connected to WIFI, didn't work. The pain seared, like a shot tearing through him and he began to panic. Surely there was internal bleeding, the water in him was replaced by blood. This pain wasn't normal, he thought something is wrong. He yelled out, *call 911*, and a woman opened her window, telling him to shut up, that it was 1:30 am and that he need to take his crackhead ass home. He tried to yell *please* but his body was too tired, shutting down to conserve energy. Eventually a cop rode by, and by then he was slumped over, breathing slowly, tears wetting through his shirt.

When the doctor comes in, she tells us that a clavicle fracture is common for children and teens, as the collarbone doesn't harden until your twenties, but that it's an unusual spot for a healthy adult to break in.

I look over at him, thin and knobby under his blanket. His shoulders jut out. Papa is not even sixty, but his body is deflated, tired. His length has permanently curled inward—his hips, knees, shoulders, and head are tight, solid spheres.

Healthy adult.

The doctor says that when he fell, his left clavicle took the brunt of it, and broke right through. Papa explained to her that he tried to catch his fall, reaching his left hand out and using his right to cushion his chest from the pavement.

The doctor tells us that this is why Papa needs surgery, that there had been enough pressure for a clean break. She explained that the collarbone connects to his breastbone's upper area, which connects to his shoulder blade and that the clavicle connects the arm to the body, therefore any movement will cause excruciating pain. "Uh, yeah, that's a little obvious," he responds, and they chuckle softly together. She says she'll need to realign the bone with screws and pins to the middle of the bone.

"Slow up, slow down, screws?" She nods and he asks, "And how long am I gonna be out for?"

"Best case, six to eight weeks for the bone to heal around the screw, to allow movement and use without pain. Unfortunately, we had a few emergency traumas come in, so we'll have to wait one more day. I'm sorry." She turns to me and nods at the menu Nurse Jess put back, "He can go ahead and order an early dinner." Papa tries to sit up a bit straighter, and winces loudly from the pain. With his uninjured hand he reaches for his shoulder. The hand of the injured side is holding onto his ribcage, his gown shifts and I can see his collarbone is a deep purple, the bruise looks brushed on, in its shade and velvety thickness.

"We're lucky it didn't hit any nerves. I'll come back in the morning before surgery," the doctor said. She smiled with a closed mouth and left, closing the curtain behind her.

"Do you want to order food?" I ask.

"Nah, I'll wait, it's only 4. I think I'll close my eyes."

And so do I, we both let the exhaustion take over.

I wake up to Papa chewing a starburst, his eyes squinted at the harsh fluorescent lighting. He tilts his head upward and says, "Oh, yeah, I remember when you fell," he says, his voice gummy from the candy, "when you were just a little kid." Papa nods up and down, remembering his knee colliding into my collarbone.

"Hey, feel this," he says, gripping his right wrist. I move to sit on the end of his bed and reach out to hold his wrist. I can almost close my thumb and pointer finger around it—knobby and too small. He was wide awake, just hours out of surgery, just finishing his first post-surgery meal.

"What am I feeling?" I ask.

"This is where I dislocated it."

"From this fall?"

"No silly, are you listening? When I was a kid playing ball. It literally broke as I caught a ball in the air."

"I didn't know that."

"Yeah, we played it all the time, or craps in the street. Man, my mother was so angry." He snorted softly.

I rubbed his wrist until he moved his hands away. Papa began to re-arrange his tray. He was calm from the painkillers. The nurse came in to check his vitals. The doctor had already come by and said the surgery went "exceptionally well." I laughed to myself when the doctor said so. Despite the way Papa treats his body, it seems to show up for him over and over again.

"Throw that away, will you?" Papa said, pointing to an empty cranberry juice container. "And this too," he said, nodding toward a Ricola wrapper. He moved his water and cup to the edge of his tray, aligned with his phone. He kept the candy I brought—Now & Laters and Starburst—in a pile on the other edge. He wiped down the rest of the tray with a napkin, and asked me to throw it away, and to move the tissue box back to the counter.

"What if you need a tissue?" I said with a smirk.

He shooed me away, looking up at the news and changing the channel. His left arm was in a sling, and he happily ate the last of his Jell-O with his right. The clouds outside move in rapid speed, the wind pushing them out of view before I could get a good look. We're both tired. We were up all night; the nurses keeping Papa up, and him, me.

"Hey, where's your necklace?" Papa asked.

"What?"

"Your chain, my ball."

"Oh, it's at home," I say, stumbling on my words. "The chain broke, I have to get it fixed."

He says nothing to this.

"Throw this away, will you?" He says, holding up the empty Jell-O container. He moved the tray to the side and lowered the bed. "And turn off the lights please?"

I tuck the blanket around the side I'm near. I sit watching *Everybody Loves Raymond*, zoning out until Nurse Jess comes in a few hours later to check his vitals.

* * *

A few days later, I go back to Philly. When I get home, I can still smell the hospital on me. The doctor and hospital social worker said he'd need rehab, that Papa couldn't live alone and take care of himself. The social worker explained that the state would pay for it. He didn't want to, but I begged him to go, scared for the what ifs. They would move him in a day or two.

"Go home for a bit, you have work, I'll be here," he said, and added, "just come back."

I said of course, "I promise."

After Papa and I used to play basketball, he'd tell me to drop the ball, to squeeze my entire body. I'd laugh at him shaking and squeezing. "Papa, you're shaking!" I'd scream, laugh.

"Come on, squeeze!" He'd say, smiling. And I would. We'd laugh and squeeze until he yelled, "okay, now release!" And we would and our bodies would shake and then settle, both of us floating off the ground an inch.

I lay on a yoga mat in the center of my living room and stretch out on the ground like a star. I work, joint by joint to release it. I try to think about each body part, to see it as mine, but my mind drifts and I let my eyes grow distant, fixed on nothing. My lower back and knee ache, and there is a headache coming, the pounding still distant. I ask my body for relief, but the plea gets stuck in the crevice between gums and tooth. Much of me does not make it past this point, past the dregs. I try to inhale and instead I shudder. I think of Papa, who will need more care than before, and my mouth clamps. As I work to try to relax my jaw, it stays shut so that nothing can slither in. I built a too-thick door with my veiny, bumpy tongue, keeping everything locked within my sharp teeth. I had done this for so long my body learned to function around it. My wish was to open as wide as the full moon, my tongue like a passing cloud that cuts across the moon's midriff; my wish was to feel every part of my body at once.

San Antonio de Padua, patron saint of the single ladies

Paloma Nieto

November 5th

Perhaps you invoked San Antonio, through retched loneliness, and prayers whispered into the void. *Send me something good.*

Perhaps for once, you were heard.

Just look at the wealth of new and miraculous matches on your dating apps. Matches of quality, of caliber. You spend hours looking at the profiles and crafting clever messages. You ask these men to send voice notes, then wake up at dawn to masturbate to the sound of their voices. More aroused than you have been in months, you play them on a loop and run out your vibrator's battery. The truth is, it's been forever since you've been touched, and even longer since you've been touched in any way that gives you pleasure. You can already imagine it: the warmth of another body in your bed all winter long, someone to nurse through the flu, perhaps even a Christmas gift. You thank San Antonio, lighting a candle and placing a flower by its base.

But by the end of the week, none of the conversations, so promising at first, have converted into dates. One by one, the messages trickle out, until each of them disappears into silence. You've done nothing wrong, nothing that could explain this. You play out multiple scenarios in your mind.

It's possible, it just might be, that San Antonio doesn't respond well to positive reinforcement.

Look at you now. You, who always found the spirituality and attachment to mysticism from back home, primitive, and provincial. Look at you, turning the statue upside down, wrapping its eyes, binding it with strings.

You catch yourself and think: *I'm losing my fucking mind.*

* * *

October 25th

Rewind: San Antonio appeared in your apartment one cold fall morning. After opening what seemed like a care package, you simply sit dumbstruck on the floor of your Bed Stuy studio walk-up staring at a 15-inch tall clay statue. The statue of a Saint, to be precise. A brown tunic, bald head, baby Christ on one arm, and a bunch of lilies on the other: San Antonio de Padua. You ruffle around the box to see if there is anything else—spices, sweets, maybe a delayed birthday present. There is only a brief note:

I thought this should be with you now; I am sure he will work miracles.
Love,
Tia Rossy

You look around. There is no one to text, not a single confidant to say: isn't this ridiculous?

Your American friends—a generous use of the term—would squint their nice white liberal eyes, full of cultural openness and acceptance.

They would ask to learn more, to be called in: Do people pray to these clay statues in your country? Do they light little candles? Do they consider them sacred in a mythological way?

Friends from back home—also a generous use of the term after six years of loose contact—would not understand your surprise or why you're texting them.

In a way, you admire Tia Rossy's restraint. She waited until your 31st birthday to send the Saint statue that would aid old maids—solteronas—in finding husbands. You kneel in front of San Antonio, just to look at it at his eye's level. Your mother used to light candles around her collection of clay saints, bring them fresh flowers, and sew them clothes. In exchange, they granted her what she called blessings but you called luck.

Until they didn't.

* * *

October 26th

The next morning, you wake up at 10 a.m., anxiously realizing you did not set an alarm and slept in longer than what's acceptable. Then comes a worse realization: you have nowhere to be. The long pit of unstructured time looms menacingly before you. Weekends are the hardest days.

As productivity always helps you feel better, you decide to go for a run. While running, you listen to your Aunt's voice messages. Tia Rossy, your mother's younger sister, has updates on the whole family that she lists quickly. Her children are playing in the background. The noise, the rattle around her, makes you long for mess, for late and crowded Sunday lunches after mass, where children would play, men would talk, old people would sleep, and there was not a moment of peace.

Her mention of your father, and his new young wife, takes you out of your melancholy, and you are suddenly relieved to be far away.

When your mother fell sick, and your father—meandering at best, controlling at worst—decided that he needed a clean break and stopped showing up; you were less angry at him than you were at yourself. "Árbol torcido, nunca su tronco endereza," said your aunt. True—they'd be separated for years, your father waltzing in and out of your mother's life when it was convenient for him. Why, then, did you expect more from him? Why were you disappointed when, day after day, he'd fail to walk through the hospital doorway, swatting away his responsibilities as he'd swat an annoying fly?

He announced he'd knocked up one of his little girlfriends before your mother's body was cold in the ground.

Of course, you didn't go to the wedding. By then, you'd followed your aunt's advice and re-engaged in your master's program. You were nearing the end at the heavy recruitment phase, where consultancies that will Change The World put you through a grueling machinery of interviews and case studies (Company X wants to start exporting butterflies. What is the expected market size? What are their estimated distribution costs?) This gave you the perfect excuse. Everyone back home understood that you were off doing Important Things that would bring Big Money.

Exhausted but full of endorphins, you indulge in a 400-500 calorie bagel sandwich and sit on a park bench to scroll through Social Media. A group of women from Grad School have posted Stories that show them having brunch a few blocks away. Isn't that what good Western women do on the weekends? Their church: debrief their sexual escapades over bottomless mimosas and provide each other with validation on their physical appearance and psychological fortitude to endure the grueling dating market. A ritual of devotion towards each other, filled with its chants and prayers (Be a Girls' Girl; Women Supporting Women.)

You, alone: a heathen.

* * *

A buzz from your cell phone is an alarm reminder to go home and get ready for a date with Kevin (32 y/o). He's an app designer working for the biggest Social Media Company in the world. He owns a dog and used to row, as stated in his dating app profile, supported by photographic evidence. He's been texting you on and off for a few weeks, his lagging responses barely enough to keep you hopeful but not to avoid a feeling of futility.

Yet, you stand up and start doing your hair, first straightening it and then curling it back into loose soft waves. Finding love, or at least, a warm kind body, is a task that should be taken with the same industriousness dedicated to a job. Before leaving the house, you jot down the data for this date in a tracking spreadsheet. You've given yourself SMART goals:

1) Go on three dates a week.

2) Respond to all the messages of men that fulfill a checklist of essential characteristics (see footnote) and give them four dates before

allowing yourself to cut communication.

3) Ignore one orange flag before each date.

Your summary statistics don't seem good, but it's hard to tell as there aren't many sources to compare them to. What you've found in the few peer-reviewed papers on the topic is this: Men of all ethnicities are three times less likely to swipe right on Latina women than they are on white and Asian women (this trends worse for Black women). These differences are statistically significant—and depressing.

Your qualitative evidence is also depressing.

Over the past few months, you've gone on dates with a man who asked if you've ever been skinnier, one who asked no questions at all, one who demanded you pee on him, another who worked for a big hedge-fund who waved the waitress away saying: "She won't have anything to eat. I don't buy food on the first date. At the rate I go out, it gets expensive."

Perhaps Kevin will be good. Perhaps he'll find you funny, interesting, attractive. He'll have a clean apartment, interests, friends. Maybe he'll talk about his family and kiss you softly by the fountain.

You sit on one of the park benches, headphones on and no book, as he doesn't seem like the kind of guy who would like that. You spot him and pretend not to.

Please, God, let this be a good date, you pray, once more, into the empty universe.

You look at the trees, trying to seem at ease and distracted. The leaves are changing, now taking on bright tones of yellow and orange. The seasonal window to find a partner is closing quickly.

After what seems like more than enough time, you discreetly look up, only to find Kevin looking around, perplexed. Tapping him on the shoulder, your worst fears materialize: he's disappointed. Here you are in the flesh: much stockier, leggier, and rougher features than he was led to believe from the kind angles in your pictures. He doesn't say anything, but you see his pupils contracting, and you catch a twitch on his lips. The briefness of his questions and his curt politeness, speak volumes. The date ends one hour later in an overpriced wine bar, as he says he is sorry he had totally forgotten that he had to meet up with a friend and help him move, and he is actually in a hurry. Could you pay for drinks? He'll send a Venmo.

* * *

You arrive home 45 minutes later—starving. This was supposed to be a dinner date. As a result of a 70-hour work week, there is nothing in the fridge. You kick off your ankle heels and are tempted to sit on the floor and cry for a bit. Opening an app, you feel too sad, too weak to decide between an overpriced and insipid salad or a greasy chicken burger—when San Antonio catches your eye.

You crouch on the floor, and touch the top of the statue's head. Longing for your mother hits you so hard, you almost lose balance. The feeling worsens with the realization that the anniversary of her death was last week while you were working until two a.m. to finish the Urgent Deck for the Client.

She'd know what to say to make it all better, to make you believe that it's not you, it's them. The nostalgia runs through you now, as well as the guilt; like a sharp knife drawing a soft and painful line from your throat to your belly button.

When your mother was diagnosed, you had the impulse to go into her room and smash the Saint statues with a hammer. Should your most fervent servant be punished, you sadists? But none of the statues were of the top guy, who just hovered around, invisible, formless. You stared at the room and then retreated; held back by the memory of your father punching walls, breaking glasses, screaming profanities at minor inconveniences of life.

Then again, this wasn't a minor inconvenience.

You could feel your mother slipping away from under your grasp, each day her skin getting thinner and her face gaunter. You gripped her harder, willing her to stay in this world, willing the universe to let her be in your life just a bit longer. You clung to her with a strength that frightened you both.

Oh, willful girl. Always bending reality to your desires out of sheer tenacity. Clawing yourself out of the pit of Lima middle class, out of an extended family that expected little to none from you. You got every prize, every scholarship, every opportunity to move up. Was there anything that couldn't be achieved from the sweat of your brow?

There was.

"It's God's will," your mother said faintly after only a few months, and she let herself be pulled away, refusing treatment, refusing science. Then again, science wouldn't have made much of a difference, with a disease caught at Stage 4.

A secret: you did break a statue. The day after she died, you grabbed Santa Teresa's statue by its base and smashed it against your mother's bed frame until the room was covered in white clay powder.

Another secret: it felt good.

Your aunt found you cleaning it up.

"Go back to your master's in the US, love," she said, taking your hand. "Tell them you are done with your bereavement leave. Build a life there, like you'd planned. There is nothing for you here anymore."

But is there something for you here? Look around: On the floor of your small studio apartment—void of warmth and of any detail that betrays a personality; no photos, postcards or clutter, no signs of human connection—what is there for you here?

You text your aunt now: *Tia, how are you? I just got the package, jaja! Thank you! How are my cousins?*

She immediately replies with pictures from your cousins and four long voice notes. You don't open them, but feel a little more loved now. And so you feel the renewed strength to order food and pick up your San Antonio, and choose a place where it will not cause disruption. You walk around the apartment with it, feeling its weight in your arms. You stop by a small mantel-place in the entryway, where you feel is his place.

You stroke the cheek of the baby Jesus, who is resting peacefully in San Antonio's arms.

* * *

October 27th

Your next date of the weekend is with Matt (38 y/o); a lawyer and self-defined gym rat who looks fantastic without a shirt and in a suit. The orange flag that you choose to ignore in this case, is his initial message: *Hola Mamacita.*

Matt sends a new message that makes you hopeful: *Excited to meet you :)*

On the way out, you pet the head of the San Antonio statue, and whisper: "Thank you."

The bar Matt chose is conveniently close to your apartment. You spot him sitting at a high table in the back, and his face lights up when he sees you. He brings you a drink and asks plenty of questions. He starts talking about the terrible week he's had, and you almost feel like you have been friends for a long time.

But when you say you are a runner, he turns serious, asks if you lift weights, and explains that cardio will only make your womanly figure become boy-ish. When you stand to buy scones and he says that he does not—under no circumstances—put sugar, fat and carbohydrates in his body at the same time—you start to wonder if it was deliberate that he messed up your order of a lavender vanilla latte, bringing you black coffee with skim milk instead. After a depressing two-hours (and having somehow purchased protein-powder from his friend), you arrive home.

For some reason, you walk straight up to the mantelpiece with the San Antonio statue.

You have the clear and vibrant image of Tia Rossy coming home after a deception or a breakup and turning San Antonio upside down, with its head suspended in thick glass to keep it in place.

Your mother explained how it's done—one had to "punish" San Antonio to make him work for you and help in love. Otherwise, he wouldn't work she said, he needed some motivation. Tia Rossy would do all sorts of things as motivation. Turn it to his back, cover him with cloth, refuse to dust him.

You think of the happy chaos that surrounds your aunt now. Children running, talking, eating, everyone living and growing together. You want that life—no—you deserve that life. You take a deep breath and carefully lay the San Antonio statue down, facing the wall.

* * *

October 28th

On Monday, you rush into the large office building where you do things that will Change The World. The realization sets in: you barely talked to anyone over the weekend outside of transactions (either a date or a direct purchase of goods). Even the office small talk feels warm.

You dive yourself into your work, assigning the new associates tasks and SMART goals that you'll monitor at the end of the week. You've been promoted quickly, too quickly to make you well-liked by the other Junior or Senior Associates. Your level of productivity and dedication puts their Protestant work ethics to the test. You have a leg up over them because you don't work hard for morality; you do it out of old-fashioned Catholic guilt that cripples you inside if you slack even for a second. Both a blessing and a curse. For your supervisors, it's entirely a blessing.

Once, at a Christmas party, your white boss sang a song from Hamilton at karaoke and pointed to you with a large smile as he sang: "Immigrants! We get the job done!" Your colleagues clapped half-heartedly.

Hey! What's up?

Hi—nice to have matched, looking forward to meeting you

Yo, wanna meet up soon?

like swimming? I'm a swimmer too!

You take your laptop into a meeting room and input the data into your spreadsheet. You've overcome your natural match average by 300%, and have even got a precious and elusive Hinge Rose.

You walk out triumphant with the desire to tell one of your colleagues. But you know better. The last time you had a few extra drinks at the company happy hour, you ended up "over-sharing"—a distinctly American term to shame intimacy that hasn't been earned. Blinded by how close in age you were, you failed to notice the intern's widening eyes as you (jokingly) described Americans' lack of finesse in bed. To your horror, the following Monday, you got a stern talk from HR and were forced to take an online training course on appropriate topics to discuss in the workplace (e.g., the weather). You've never overshared— or shared—since.

Still, you aren't discouraged. The rest of the day in a haze. While attending meetings, taking notes, making small talk, typing into spreadsheets, analyzing data, and accepting more work you could possibly complete, you ponder.

Everything has remained constant over the past week. Expect one thing. One variable.

* * *

November 5th

Which leads you to that night. Slippery consciousness and violent pleasure. Perhaps you are indeed losing your mind. But the data doesn't lie, something has gone wrong. This week, none of your SMART goals have been achieved. There aren't only less messages, but also less matches than your average. You face the prospect of a whole weekend without talking to anyone.

In a fit of rage you Google: *"CIA torture strategies"*

You catch yourself and think: *I'm sick, I'm a sick, crazy person.*

Your pupils expand while watching increasingly horrid things, such as waterboarding and shock torture. You dip San Antonio in water for as long as a person could endure (though only the head so that the little baby Jesus in his arms does not suffer the same fate). In the middle of the night, you approach the statue to a lamp to scorch its ear.

Just then, your phone buzzes with a match.

You are awoken from the frenzy. You collapse on the ground, panting, and covered in the cold sweat of relief. It's quickly replaced by waves of guilt and shame as you face San Antonio. You place him neatly over the mantelpiece and whisper prayers of apology.

You quickly read the profile and the messages of your new match. Greg (33 y/o) is moderately attractive and works in tech. You quickly strike up a conversation while balancing on your toes, crouched by the mantlepiece. He asks for a date for Saturday.

You gently stroke San Antonio. The clay is soft against your fingers, and you feel a tingle of pleasure. You kiss the top of his head and whisper: "Thank you."

* * *

November 6th

You spend the next morning reviewing Greg's profile. He has responded to the "green flags" prompt, saying that he loves poetry and books. In a next prompt, he writes that his favorite writers are Kerouac, Bukowski, and Hemingway, which is the orange flag you chose to ignore.

You arrive at the bar, and the stools are high. He is a full ten inches shorter than his profile listed, but he has a beard and a man bun. There is a MeToo case in the news playing in the background. A famous actor was accused of domestic violence and a lot of evidence was presented against him. He then sued his wife for defamation. The case is televised and unbearable to watch, though it is also impossible to avoid. All month, you've scrolled through the TikTok videos making fun of the wife's testimony and have wondered what on earth could have made your algorithm misunderstand you so. You tell him this, thinking it's a clever thing to say to someone who works in tech. But he wants to talk about details of the actual case.

"It is really wild, no? All that?" he says.

"Yes, it is crazy. The way the media is feeding off this person's suffering." You mean the woman's.

"That should show her, though. You can't just go around spreading lies with no consequences. If there is no accountability, then no one is safe." He means, to your horror, the man.

You stop listening after that comment. That evening, you break the rule of giving men four dates. You find a template message online to kindly and politely reject someone.

I really enjoyed spending time with you today! But I am sorry, I just don't feel the connection I am looking for. All the best! xx

He messages back almost immediately.

You sutpid cow you think I havnt seen this before? I cant believe I wasted my time with you to get this stupid ass template response…

You lie in bed that night, unable to sleep. That was more unpleasant than you deserved. A chill runs through your body. Were you too swift to count him out? Your only match. Soon it will be winter, people will retreat for months into the warmth of their relationships, and your loneliness will be more tangible. Was it too much to ask? Someone to watch movies with, to tell about your day, to cook for.

Your father once told you that you'd never find anyone to put up with you. "Difficult," by which he meant so competent that you'd be emasculating. It shouldn't have hurt as much as it did. A parentifiedeldest-daughter is a dirtbag-father's worst nightmare. The Joker to his Batman. The Doña Florinda to his Chavo. But although he said it out of spite, as part of your endless battles for control over the household, you know that he truly believed that someone like you was cursed to be alone. His words resonate in your mind now.

You wrap yourself up in a blanket but can't seem to warm up. Why have things been going so poorly lately? Your weekly statistics were never great but never this bad. The only explanation that crosses your mind: San Antonio doesn't respond to niceties but doesn't like this specific type of punishment either. He's retaliating.

Time to escalate. Someone was to show him who's boss.

* * *

This was never the plan, but what else would work? You conclude you've gone too modern with your strategies. After all, he was born in the 14th century.

You open Google and type: *"Spanish Inquisition - torture tactics"*

What comes out is absolutely awful. It makes you recoil. Still, you take notes in a tiny notebook.

You do things you're not proud of. You're even less proud of how much they excite you. In the haze of two a.m. you take a knife with a short tip and make small incisions in the toes that overflow from the tunic of the San Antonio, and on its shoulder blades. Crying, you beg him to help. You then leave San Antonio in the freezer.

You masturbate frantically for hours while playing the voice notes of the men who have ghosted you and imagining hurting them in a way that brings you both pleasure. A slap, a spit, a whip. You come again and again, ecstasy compounding.

Do you know why violence feels good? Because it tastes like both power and abandonment. *Is this control?* you ask yourself, *Is this rapture? Is this grace? Is this what we fought for, the third wave feminists, for our own opportunity to slap men in the ass and hear them moan?*

You fall asleep at dawn, drunk off power and craze. The limits to your sanity melt away. There are no witnesses to your life and your choices, and so it seems that the memory of your actions can vanish with enough effort.

Shame vanishes, too.

* * *

November 7th
When you wake, a match buzzes in your phone, and you hungrily inspect it. Anthony (35 y/o) has long lashes and eye-lined hazel eyes. He has a languid air about him. He is alone in each of his pictures, staring into the distance or at the camera.

Messages come in quickly. He writes in full sentences, and refreshingly, uses punctuation.
Hello. You have a beautiful smile.

You set a date for that evening.

At home, after a long hot shower, you defrost Saint Antonio and pat him on the head. Last night worked.

Anthony writes: *I could come over to your apartment and cook for you.*

Normally, this is not something you would have agreed with. Dateline has taught you to know better. But this time, they seem like the most attractive words ever written.

He arrives at exactly eight p.m. He greets you with a kiss on the cheek. You know his smell: incense and rose-water cologne. He seems to know his way around your house. He swiftly unpacks groceries and opens drawers to get utensils. He chops with his left hand.

He doesn't talk much about himself. Or much at all. He asks questions that prompt you to share. Even overshare. Stories that you would normally leave out until the sixth or tenth date, though you have not progressed that far in too long. Like when you and your mother bought a whole carton of mangoes, ate them all over a weekend, and then were sick together for a week.

You laugh and he smiles kindly.

What would your mother have made of him? "Look for someone who has kind eyes. Someone who'll understand you," she used to say.

After too much wine, your eyelids begin to feel heavy.

He clears the table, and hovers over you. The smell of his body is intoxicating and pulls you to him. "Shall we go to bed?"

You smile, and say: "Yes, please."

You undress him. He watches you undress. He has a bandage on his foot. When he turns, you see he also has injuries in his back. He winces when you touch them but tells you to carry on, and this makes you wet.

He lets you guide him around your body, you whisper what you want, what you need. At one point, he looks into your eyes.

"Do you want to hurt me?" he asks.

You have never been more aroused. You scratch, you slap, you lick. He places your hands around his neck, and you squeeze while he enters you, and then, squeeze harder.

You come screaming and are suspended in heaven for perhaps a second or perhaps an eternity. You drift off to sleep wrapped up in his warmth, comforted by the weight and heat of his body. Your last thought is: *Thank you, Lord, for this gift.*

The next morning, you wake up peaceful and happy yet alone.

When you look around the apartment, you find the statue still on the mantelpiece, with a dark hue around its neck.

You pick up the statue and gently kiss each of its kind eyes. Cradling it in your arms, you descend the four stories, and carefully place it on the stoop.

One by one, you delete the dating apps plaguing your phone, and walk into the city, lighter, satisfied, saved.

Swimmers

Sabrina Shie

Every week I go to the temple and ask Nainai if she feels like coming home yet. Every week she looks up from counting her prayer beads with a face that's like, Can't you see I'm counting my prayer beads? I can tell from how her eyebrows raise then lower and her hands start thumbing the beads in reverse, as if she's rewinding some cosmic tape recorder to the moment before I walked in.

Still, I get her. Yesterday at the swim meet, Tingting was supposed to help me count off 66 laps but she flipped the counter placard to the red END square somewhere around Lap 42, and when I strolled out of the pool with the fastest mile time California has ever seen, Coach's face was so red from screaming, I had to offer him a puff of my inhaler. Behind him college recruiters sat in the bleachers, Divisions 1 and 2 and 3 shaking their heads. Like baby, baby, baby, you are never leaving the Bay.

Tingting said she couldn't help it, she'd been too mesmerized by her boy of the week Brian walking by with his too tight speedo that always showed one inch of asscrack. She liked watching the rivulets of water slide past his hips and disappear down his wet suit.

Honestly Audrey, Tingting told me, I got bored of counting laps and started counting how many chopsticks might fit in the dark little line that pops over the water when Brian swims fly.

Sometimes Tingting is like a cat discovering tinsel.

So I wanted to tell my grandmother that I understood her pain intimately, and if I could, I would rewind to the moment Brian was picking out his little loincloth, so that maybe my best friend's eyeballs wouldn't fall out of their sockets three quarters into my race. But I know Nainai would just hand me a set of prayer beads and tell me to start counting. She'd look at me like, My baby, breathe in, breathe out. Let go of these attachments. You don't want to bring them into the next life.

Instead, I reach into my bag and pull out this week's offerings, peaches that Tingting left for me on her kitchen counter. I'm always over at her place to pick up Mom's pay stubs so we can pretend our address is actually in the good school district, you know, the kind that bothers to invite recruiters to the pool. Tingting's parents didn't have a problem affording a house here once her dad's startup (along with all the other startups) began making actual money and the mayor's campaign to get us to stop calling San Jose Tan Jose, Fob City, San Francisco's Ugly Stepsister and something more dignified like *The Capital of Silicon Valley* started making sense. I consider telling Nainai that Tingting's Taiwanese grandmother took one look at my goggle tan splashed across my sunburnt face and started muttering that dirty Mainlanders were once again coming into her house to steal her shit. Old people are always occupied by the past.

But who cares, everyone here knows all about it, especially once the tech startups started giving out so many visas that the schools flooded with immigrant tryhards and the white kids had to run for the private school hills. Our principal even hired a former 49er to come tell us why we ought to give a shit about historical institutions like football tryouts and Homecoming royalty, but even then, we had other histories to worry about.

Like one time our best sprinter Jane refused to get into Tingting's Toyota Camry because her grandparents never got any apologies from Japan, so we showed up to Sectionals without her and Coach asked us how we planned on swimming a relay with only three people. Like one time, Tingting and I got into it over what kind of Chinese is more superior: the kind that's so fake and cheap that even the character for love is written without the symbol for heart or the kind that takes a hundred years and a hand cramp to write out "shut the fuck up"? Our team's breastroker Annie yelled at us to stop hogging the wall and start swimming, and when we ignored her, she said us East Asians taking up so much space must be why all the pho on the westside was so watered down. She kicked at us with her fatass frog legs but got Kevin square in the stomach instead and he started spewing his lunch all over Lane 3. For a week after, all of us swore yam noodles were slithering up our butts every time we did a flipturn. Like one time, Daniel showed up to practice with an American flag screen-printed across his suit because he wasn't like us uncivilized freaks, his whole family had properly converted as soon as they got here and he'd pray to Jesus for all our salvations. For that, we all held him down while our team captain pantsed him and slung his speedo in one smooth arc onto the backstroke flags. Now Daniel wears two suits on the pool deck.

Us kids couldn't help it, you know? At the pool, the history the older generations stuffed us with slipped out, the way you just can't stop farts from surfacing on water. At the pool, we paddled around like little

English broadcasters for our shit talking elders. But only at the pool did we have the space to compare notes and figure out how much was actual history and how much was our grandparents refusing to take their meds. Only at the pool could counting laps, counting strokes, counting breaths seem to dissolve the urgency and pain of all our pasts. Cause like, at the end of the day, we were still trying to spend all our money on the latest chapters of *Naruto* and *One Piece,* you know?

I watch as Nainai places the peaches on the altar in front of the statue of GuanYinPusa and lights incense for Dad, gesturing at me to pray for his safe reincarnation into the next life. Neither of us bother acting like his soul's gonna reach nirvana, no way. That's if you've really left this Earth peacefully, with no unfinished business. But my aunt in China once told me, this guy really worked 80 hours a week for that startup, and did I really think a little heart attack was gonna stop him from collecting his check? She said Dad was the kind of guy who was so good at gambling, he plucked the gold capped molar out of her mouth while she was asleep and came back with enough cash to get her a whole mouth of metal. This life was just a bad bet, she said once over the phone. He'll be back for sure.

And before Nainai left Mom and me to live at the temple, she said that any parent always comes back for their kid in one form or another, which is why she's here day in, day out, praying for her son. But I don't know, it's been four years and I'm just wondering, do these karmic cycles really ever end? Instead, I pray for something real, like lightning, so practice gets canceled and I can sleep in.

* * *

Coach is busting our asses today. He's like, Audrey, what happened last week is *never* happening again. So he put us on four miles on a diminishing interval: first mile on 45 minutes, next one on 40, then 35, you get it. I don't know how to tell him we already lost count five minutes ago. See, Tingting had the idea to count off our laps with the clock, except the water polo players reset their shot clock, which somehow reset every clock on deck. And I knew we were never getting back on track when I saw her sitting on the wall blowing kisses at Brian, and Jane's hot pink swim cap started leading the pack instead. Everyone knows sprinters can't count higher than 8.

I can tell it's gonna be one of those days, where time loses all form and you're just out there floating on a six-beat flutter. You start thinking thoughts that lead nowhere, questions without any answers, like: In my last life, was I a tiger or a horse? And you start imagining yourself as the happiest horse galloping through the Mongolian plains, or at least, a powerful tiger springing over the peaks of HuangShan. And once you're hitting that flow state and you're lapping that one freshman with the long ass legs who really ought to be running track, you know damn well you must have been a motherfucking swordfish, that's how smoothly you're chopping up everyone's waves. And sometimes even, when you can feel the collective consciousness of the universe on your fingertips, that's when the real deep shit comes out like, What exactly did The Pharcyde mean by "can't keep runnin' away" in their hit 1995 single?

But in the middle of practice, Tingting pulls up beside me, and we push off the wall at the same time. We're gliding so closely together I can see glimpses of her shoulder blades, spot my air bubbles gathering in her back dimples. I let her pass me by, but it's too late, shit's off tempo, Fatlip's freshly split from Pharcyde, and now I'm breathing too much on my right, as if more air is going to save me from being pulled into Tingting's current. I start wondering things like how's it possible the rest of us have the kind of chlorine-bleached hair that looks hella fried, while Tingting's got golden flecks in her blonded out hair, the kind that makes the ABGs put down their Henny flasks to ask for her stylist's number? Or how is it possible the rest of us have cap tans that look like we just went to Korea to get our hairlines lowered, the kind that makes the ABGs put down their half-sweet, less-ice boba to show us stylists who can cut good bangs? And somehow, Tingting doesn't even have a goggle tan. Or how come she gets to drive to school and I've gotta haul ass to Caltrain? Or how come some Nainais get to sit around all day and judge while other Nainais spend hours at the altar releasing any feeling at all? Or how come some dads drop a million on a house and other dads drop dead?

I push forward faster and faster because these questions are all converging into the one that always comes up when my breathing's whack, my count's wrong, my body's lagging behind my brain, the one that's like, how many rebirths, how many renewed lifetimes, do you think it would take to get to a life as good as Tingting's?

You see? Losing count means I'm racing against a past that can't be changed, and I know it's a loser's game, but I don't stop swimming until Tingting grabs me by the ankle and is like, Practice is over Michael Phelps, and Coach is like, Audrey, these times could get us to State.

* * *

No matter what, Tingting takes care of me more than anyone and I'm grateful for that. She tells me the hard truths nobody else does. Like right now, she's telling me I'm driving her car the same way I swim, as in, I'm always edging right up to other cars because I'm, and I quote, too chicken shit to pass anyone. We watch as the guy in front confirms this by flipping us off. Tingting returns the bird just as quick, and goes right back to patting gloss on her lips, all while saying, I could feel you on my ass that whole practice, like, if I started swimming any slower, I just know your head would've jammed right up my vag, goddamn. Why didn't you just take the lead?

We're stopped at the lights, waiting to turn left onto 280. I'd shown up late to morning practice and Coach was so pissed, he made the team run laps around the track for every minute late (bitches kept grumbling if they wanted to sign up for track, they would've signed up for track, and Tingting was like, But do bitches want stitches? And you know they don't). Then he asked if he could count on me being on time for these last three weeks of the season. I can never tell what kind of fairytale Coach is living in. Everyone knows Caltrain only runs once an hour, and that's without counting all the delays caused by rewiring the train to run electric. Progress never stops in this city, except when it comes to getting me to practice. But Tingting was like, I'm gonna help you get your license. And how could I say no to that?

Cause let's face it, who else is gonna teach me? I asked Mom if she could, but she's hardly ever home. She used to fly SF to LA and I'd see her every night, but now Mom does the transpacific routes: SFO to PEK and PVG. Two days in the air, one day in China. Two days in the air, one day in the Bay. If Mom's not flying into the future, she's hurtling half a day into the past. And if you're so lost in time, how're you gonna teach anyone to drive?

I ran this question by Nainai once during my weekly visits after asking her my usual one about coming home. You're not really supposed to talk in the prayer hall, but you can barely hear anyone over the Buddha chants blasting over the speakers anyways. I actually run a ton of questions by her each week, and believe it or not, she has that same response for every one of them, the one that's like: My baby, there's no gaining or losing time, it just is. Come count with me, your time will come when it comes.

Secretly, I think Nainai's only like this because she's tapping out of this lifetime and she's ready to go, the way old people are. I bet before, when Dad immigrated us out to the Bay, she put down her prayer beads for once and hollered something like, Hot dog! I wouldn't know, I was a baby. But when she moved to the temple, instead of watching soap operas at home like anyone else, she said it was because she could feel decades of people's unmet desires drifting up from the land, that it gave her stomach aches and made her sick. Mom told her it was just American dairy. I try not to want too much.

So Tingting is as good a teacher as anyone. I merge us onto the freeway and we head toward the heart of the city. She tells me to forget the rules, like putting your hands on the 10 and 2 or staying under the speed limit. Driving is about feeling the flow, she declares. She goes through her CDs and slots in Britney, while I work so hard at forgetting, we start drifting onto the shoulder. When Tingting feels me anxiously hitting the brakes, she tells me to stay on beat, but my driving ankle can barely hold it together and we drip right past the off ramp to the mall with its historic haunted house, past the giant yellow rubber duck sitting afloat the Children's Discovery Museum, like some ten foot tall guide beckoning toward a future that could have been. Tingting keeps musing about whether or not she'll miss these places once we graduate, but I'm too busy concentrating on pop princesses asking me, Baby, baby, how do you want it to be?

Tingting's talking to herself louder now, saying something about how she's only got one life, she's gonna do as much as she can. We can always come back here, you know, she says, as she grabs the wheel to straighten me out, and tells me to start with the basics, which is to stay in the present or else we'd both get clocked. So I do. Tingting guides me past construction sites for incoming business complexes, past billboards advertising big potential. We ripple down exit ramps and she tells me when to swerve, if only to avoid potholes and pigeons and jaywalking pedestrians. We drive the wrong way down one-way streets (but we only make that mistake once).

Sometimes Tingting is so confident, I can tell she's put some numbers on her soul. That she's lived through a thousand human reincarnations and that's why she's so sure everything eventually works out. Flying through downtown with Tingting's full attention on me, I find myself believing her.

* * *

At afternoon practice, I notice Tingting isn't really talking to Brian much and I wonder if she's moved onto someone new. When I ask her what's up, she climbs on top of the diving blocks and loudly proclaims the tongue is a muscle that must be trained—that's why kissing men who insist on pushing one language onto the world could never be satisfying. Then she swan-dives into the pool before Coach can yell at us to shut up and start swimming already. I follow after her, but not before catching the look on Brian's face that's like, is your best friend calling me a banana? I almost feel for him, because it's not his fault his parents are second gen and the extent of his Chinese is pointing his finger at restaurant menus. Besides, the way Tingting is, she'll probably have a new guy picked out by the end of the week. Although let's be honest, it's not like I can speak the language that much better than Brian. I only know enough to talk to Nainai.

I can feel my thoughts spinning out the way they do when I'm getting lost in the laps, and when I finally look up, I'm surprised to see it's dark. Daylight Savings must have ended, otherwise how could practice last long enough for Coach to set down his stopwatch and start picking out the warmest parka from the bleachers? The perimeter of yellow orbs lighting up the pool walls are making the water all aquamarine and it's taking me back to the night Nainai came to practice after Dad died. She took one look at us kids flinging our arms and legs around in the air and said she could see the afterlife following us, their shadowy imprints clear proof of souls swimming through space. The next day, she tried sewing her jade pendant into my suit.

My goggles keep fogging up, and I can't make out much except shadows bobbing on the pool floor. Maybe Nainai's right and Dad's soul is doing the doggy paddle just ahead of me. Maybe, if he's really there, he could answer all these questions I've got about life. Like, if anyone could add an hour anywhere, then does that mean time's never been real? And if time's never been real, then was it too late to ask if he's okay with me leaving him behind? Some questions I wish he'd asked me first.

After practice, Tingting says she can see my tongue flapping up and down out of my mouth while I'm swimming, like it's doing its own drills, like it's trying to say something. She tells me she thinks it's creating too much drag because my splits are getting slower.

On the pool deck above, Coach wants to know exactly what my future plans are. There's only one more meet with the recruiters left, he says, all bundled up in Tingting's maroon parka.

But I tell him I'm just trying to keep count. These are my times.

* * *

Tingting says the best place to practice parking is at the drive-in theater. First, she says, you buy a ticket and practice parking in front of the screen. Then you watch a movie. Then you move the two orange cones separating one screen's parking area from another and practice again, until the guy running the theater comes over and tries to get a pic of your license plate to put on his Wall of Fame.

Tonight, they're playing *Kung Fu Hustle*, which we've already seen, but we'll watch it again because it's such a classic. Besides, we've only ever seen pirated versions, the kind that everyone's uncles smuggle over from China in thin plastic Styrofoam for disc protection, not that it helps because they're always importing the Shanghai peanut nougat as well, the one that everyone's mom loves but is so rock hard, eating it undoes anything our middle school braces ever hoped to achieve, and fully scratches out where Sing finally figures out what the Buddha's been trying to tell him this whole time. But who cares, I'm pretty sure we could watch this shit forever, 1940s gangsters discovering the Power of Kung Fu.

Tingting's right that I need parking practice though, because I get the angle all wrong. Sitting in my mom's Honda Odyssey, we're more or less at 45 degrees, taking up three spots, and facing Screen 4 instead of Screen 2. I look over at Tingting for help, but she's distracted, texting something on her pink Motorola Razr. I peek over her shoulder and see her texting Brian that she's signed to swim at Caltech.

I gape at her. But you suck at math, I tell her. Science, even more. Of course, people left all the time for school and work, but I'm having a hard time imagining Tingting swimming somewhere without me. The screen in front of us keeps showing the wrong images, not martial arts, but high schoolers at a summer camp. I turn on the radio to get the right audio, but we're out of range and all the scanner picks up is the opening sequence of *Kung Fu Hustle* on Screen 2. The mismatched sounds fill the space between Tingting and me.

I can't help it, Tingting tells me, burying her face in her hands. She also tells me she's signing with Brian, that she's never cared about someone else this much before, and that she doesn't care what anyone thinks, she knows it'll work out. She's looking staunchly at the screen when she says, I'm going where he goes.

In front of us, the scene is showing two girls arguing at a bar. I recognize Natasha Lyonne, but not the other one. Even so, their fight is full Cantonese, both of them bragging about how fast their punches are, how powerful their next moves are going to be. Then, the two girls lean inward and kiss each other.

Pow! Pow! Pow!!

I've watched enough kungfu movies to easily follow the rhythms of every scripted blow, but as the girls tenderly cup each other's faces instead, I'm too overwhelmed to say anything except, What is happening?

Tingting shrugs and gestures toward the big movie board where the sign says SCREEN#4: BUT I'M A CHEERLEADER. We sit in silence, even after the credits roll—Tingting texting on her phone every five minutes or so and me, with this recurring thought that this has gotta be my first human life because there's no way I've experienced this kind of feeling again and again before, is there?

Sometimes I wish I'd been reborn into something easier to love, like the two little moles under Tingting's right eye or the beads that Nainai's always caressing.

* * *

The day of the season's final meet, I skip school to visit Nainai at the temple. I can tell she hears me approaching because her fingers start slowing on the beads, like she's getting ready for my usual interruption, but when I only sit quietly beside her, she eventually stops counting, then turns to me with this face full of concern, like what's going on? Did something happen? She treads out of the prayer area, with her kneeling pillow tucked under her arm, before returning with a bottle of Kikkoman and dousing my tongue in soy sauce.

Dad once told me this is one of her methods to reduce inflammation. I know it works because he said Nainai caught Yeye with the auntie down the street, so she dumped a kettle of boiling water on him followed by an entire gallon of soy sauce, and nothing happened except all his wrinkles got smoothed out. So I don't mind the salt flooding my mouth, but for the first time, I do notice the way her hands tremble, her body moving like an ancient being through time.

I try answering Nainai as honestly as I can, which is that I think everything is about to change. She looks at me with her usual expression, before handing me her prayer beads. Come count with me, she says. How do you think anyone ever got past anything in this life? So I sit there with her, my hands moving through the motions as my thoughts drift toward everyone I've ever known, and the distance their souls have traveled, through continents, through generations, through each other's lives, all the karmic cycles it took for our paths to converge here, despite how heavy the past hangs in the city of the future.

I open my eyes, letting the light of my present life soften the edges of my vision. What can we do? What can any of us do? I plant both feet on the ground and slowly stand up. Then I grab my shit and head out to swim.

Spell It Different, Take Up Space

Naima Ramos-Chapman

I'm on a mission for some plants. Moving plants in and a man out. I want some plants like the ones my ma had running up and around and through her house. They ran the place. She even named 'em. There was George who was older than me, got so big he burrowed a little hole in the ceiling of our rent-controlled apartment so when my sis and I would walk home in the afternoon from school I'd look up at our window on the sixth floor on Ocean Avenue in Flatbush; there I'd see George's long branch arm reach out and wave down at us through the red and brown brick.

So forget that it was too hot, about 96 degrees outside, and sticky–so sticky my thighs were tussling. I trudged up Nostrand Avenue with a rusty cart in my Edwardian era slip feeling like at any moment I could be taken in the right way by the right man. The swish of the white fabric tugging at my waist made me think of that scene in the movie *Impromptu* that I'd rewind as a teenager on VHS over and over again. Chopin, played by Hugh Grant, rubbed the highly independent Judy Davis as George Sand's right tit on his way to take a piss. I wanted to be touched like Sand—in passing. Have lovers of the right kind. Where a man would want me for the way I moved through the world without him, maybe in spite of him, rather than the way I could move my world for him.

But on Nostrand Ave. in Bed-Stuy, all that was moving was me and my rusty shopping cart whose rattling, close on my heels, reminds me of Sundays spent at the coin-op laundromat where all that stood between my mom and I were billowed sheets still warm from the dryer that ate our quarters and greasy McDonald breakfasts she'd treat us to for getting up so early. Washrag-to-face kind of early, tongue-on-thumb to wash the sleep out your face kind of early. You could say we were close. Close enough that when I was in danger I'd see life flash between my mama's thighs.

I find my way crossing Atlantic Avenue on Nostrand through the throng of *Final Call* pamphleteers, past the Senegalese hair braiding shops, not too far from Bling Bling Nails, alone when I hear these POP, POP, POPS. They are too slow and too close, out of time with the metaphorical "bombs bursting through air" pyrotechnic poetry we all gave license to watch stream across our sky annually on the fourth–a sound that now pricked puckered shoulders and muddied foreheads on the daily with no reprieve in sight. POP! An impatient thought tells me I am having an aneurysm brought on by a cop city hell bent on unravelling the last strands of rational thought I hold tighter than a Double Dutch rope. POP! Naturally, I blame all of humanity. Respectable plants like George find a way to grow in the dark believing it will reach the sun in due time, but people? They *fight* to make sunlight their beck and call girl. POP! I just wanted some fucking plants to talk to. POP! And my ex's film canisters out of my refrigerator. POP! Before he worked up the nerve to return from Los Angeles with a sister wife I never asked for. When I confessed to him I couldn't come from our sex, he said, "That's because you're blocked and you haven't dealt with the root issue. Your dad."

"Oh," I said.

Before I can run in a zig zag—because that's how you do it, I see this young dude's knees buckle right in front of me. I see he's about six feet away but I don't want to see his face. It's enough to hear him falling and screaming in a pool of his own fucking blood. I don't wait to be a witness, I don't wait to be with him or for him or against him. You pay attention more than you have to and you go down too. They die inside you over and over and over again.

Once was enough.

First time it was Polo's homie who was left in the street for hours by police for everybody in the neighborhood to see. A chalked plan around his body, erasing him with sheets, lessons pointing straight at us. I try to outrun lessons I wouldn't teach. I sprint in double time, diving into a Fedex store, shoving the delivery guy out of my way and warning him to not go outside. Of course, he doesn't listen. I dive, dolphin kicking through towers of packages, holding tight to my shopping cart all the way into the backroom. Safe. It's ok to want this ass on a floor behind boxes out of harm's way.

A woman comes to stand over me and laughs, "What are you doing here?"

I tell her what I saw. She's impressed I still have my shopping cart and then leaves me to join the delivery guy outside and see what's going on for herself. I shake my head, roll my eyes. She too becomes a stupid witness.

Before I was born, my ma did a stint as a bodyguard for Black Power revolutionaries and she says you wait and listen. Find another way to see what's going on through reflective surfaces or in the faces of people;

you watch their body speak. You take a bullet only if you have to but if you see it coming around the corner that's even better. For her, hypervigilance is passing down a nervous system that never sleeps where in every crevice of existence lies a threat to be managed, a virtue. I check my Citizens App: 20-something-year-old murdered by rival motorcycle gang. The young man was rushed to the hospital. It was reported that even on his deathbed he refused to rat on who shot him.

* * *

We all go, but the how seems key for some reason I still don't have words for. Like how you die will either bring shame to your family's name or not and names mean a lot to mine. My name means delicate intangible gift in Arabic. In Hebrew, pleasantness of spirit. Naima—a name that is often mispronounced leading to an awkward dance of either letting people off the hook in saying it right or teaching them how to hold the i in their mouth properly thus holding me properly. Nah-E-Ma. Its melodic yet cumbersome nature seems to be the point—a funny line drawn in the sand by my father to test outsiders and garner whether they cared enough to listen attentively, ask good questions,and labor to find a way for us to speak the same languages.

My name would often conjure deeper conversations on religion and history and eventually land on jazz. I would nod knowingly after a stranger told me excitedly as if this was the first time I'd hear I was named after the John Coltrane song "Naima." Coooool, I'd say mirroring back enthusiasm while keeping it deep down to myself that I thought it was a shame for all that Juanita Naima Gibbs did to get Coltrane clean *she* wouldn't end up with him and instead had to live alongside this song everyone just yabbered on about. My daddy, like Coltrane, needs a Naima—someone to get him clean and to mean something. I don't think he thought through how I would feel on the other side of his hope once it died, a version of me with it.

I hear sirens bemoan and see the crowds on the corner grow thicker, more confident that the worst is over. I'm five feet, eleven inches and laying on the cool floor in FedEx but no one could care less so I peel myself up and leave through the door from which I came before the lady returns to wonder why I'm still hiding. Shopping cart empty, I take the long way home and without my fucking plants.

I wanna call someone. My spit tastes metallic, my skin is hot, the sky looks down at me indifferently as the speed of everything splays like an accordion. Somehow no one is moving fast enough away from danger or slow enough to see what's really going on. I scroll through my phone. Who loves me? Who could understand me?

I hit up my emotionally unavailable back-up husband. I plan to move him in one day when it's right. The last letter I wrote him confessing my love he responded to with a text days later, "I can't be your lover but I can be your friend."

Life finds a way like Jeff Goldblum says in *Jurassic Park* so I find a way through our trips to the shore that he says are not dates. Even when we hold hands? Doesn't remember the next day and the walls around his heart that expand out as girlfriends come and go, they the shape of water smoothing a way for me to see into him and stay. He doesn't answer my call so I leave a voice message. Hours pass. I follow up with a voice note so he knows I need him. No reply, and since there's nothing to read I read between the lines. Clearly, he must not have gotten my call. I send a text after that and to kill time I open a bottle of wine. Ok maybe one more. Just two bottles, not another text. I put on my red wig I call "Slaytina" and call my homegirl so she can come scoop me.

"Bet," she says.

We attend a banging block party called "Stuyami," def worthy of a feature on World Star Hip Hop. I'm checking my phone...still crickets. Only a few hours have passed since the last text. Over music that is too loud, I tell my bestie who's asking what's wrong that I almost died… but that I'm "fine."

She suggests we book an AirBnB all the way in Jersey for a weekend getaway.

YASSS roadtrip!

New Jersey becomes my idea of sanctuary.

* * *

When we get to Jersey, I find a nice grassy spot in the backyard; there's a cute chicken coup nearby. *Cluck cluck* go the hens. It's giving farm to table by a lake. I check my phone—my imaginary boyfriend who I plan to have kids with still hasn't called.

I think about my mother.…I am never not thinking about her. It takes many thoughts to land on "when people have near death experiences, they call their mothers…"

She is not that kind of mother. I look her up in my phone by her full government name because that's how she's saved. My ex thought that was weird of me—how I called her by her name. He saves his mom as

"MOMMY," now that's weird! Probably why we ain't work out.

The phone rings. She answers! Before I could even tell her what happened, she yells, "Naima if you don't pay your fucking student loans—" and in this moment I'm glad she didn't name me. She likes to tell me if she did she would have named me Mercedes…after a car. Because it's a good yelling name: Mer-ceeeeedeeeeees.

"Ma! I saw a man die; there was a shooting on Nostrand Ave,"

"Are you hurt?"

"He was right in front of me–"

"Why is Sallie Mae calling me?

"Ma! Did you hear what I said?"

"I know you saw some blood but…" Okay, acknowledgement, that's a start.

"I saw people in Greensboro massacred back in '79 by the Klan and look at me, I turned out fine."

Holy shit. What do you even say to that?

"Ma, you don't tell a kid to 'walk it off' after they survive a shooting as if it's no big deal!"

"Did you wedge yourself between cars to protect yourself when a riot breaks out—like I taught you?"

"Ma! Did you hear me? I almost died!"

I start to sob, like ugly, heaving, and huffing...sounds asthmatic because I am asthmatic.

"Ummmmm, Naima…"

"Yes, ma." I start shaking like a baby…

"Call me back after you're done crying ok?"

She tries to hang up. I've seen her cry once in her life when her mother died.

"Oooooh no you don't." I lose it. "Mom, you're going to stay on this fucking phone."

My mom is gonna *mom* today even if I have to show her. This is probably why we ain't work.

"Ma, you're gonna hear me heave and sob with snot all over my face. You're gonna provide me with emotional support because well, that's what mothers do."

She's quiet...hold up! Is this a real beat of—gasp—reflection?

I can hear her breathing; smell her thinking; two swigs of box wine down the gullet: one for me, one for her. That's how compassion works.

I take a breath and then I tell her what I would've wanted to hear, give her what she wasn't given.

"Mom. I'm sorry that happened to you. You didn't deserve that. I love you and I'd hate if anything ever happened to you or made you scared."

More silence over state lines through radio waves and electric signal. You could say we are close.

"You know…I'm not good at this kinda stuff, Naima."

She's honest. So I'm honest back.

"I know, ma."

"I saw hundreds of my friends wiped out. I slept on mattresses I had to put on the floor to avoid gunshots…but a stray bullet almost hitting my kid? Of course I'm scared. I don't know what I'd do if you got hurt."

And right there she feels me. Understands: another word for love. Should be enough but because I'm my mother's daughter I push a little more.

"So can I come home and stay for a little while I—"

"See, I knew you wanted something. Are you not paying the rent either? Damn Naima."

And she hangs up, ha!

* * *

I look out toward the Greenwood Lake in Jersey by the AirBnB. It's glassy now that the wind has calmed. The hum of mosquitos almost sounds sweet and the sun's twilight reflection seems to promise a return for another day. It smells like...Jersey. But fuck it.

* * *

My phone rings and it's my pretend boo. Finally. I answer it.

I tell him about the dead man, how I almost died but in a cool affect my mom would be proud of. I tell him it's no big deal and we hang up.

Maybe next time I'll tell him I am not so secretly in-love with him but probably not...

Because his name is heavy: blessed and cursed. Blood flow crazy now, let's reverse.

I gave him a rubber plant once and he told me it died. I wish he lied.

That he didn't name it told me everything I needed to know.

Bored of Education

Ellen Hagan

Wake up before the buzzer. Shove alarm clock across the room. Wipe eyes. Imagine being alone in a hotel room where no one wants anything from you. Buck up. Suck it up. Remember you're sleeping on the pull-out sofa while your two children share the only bedroom in the only apartment you can afford since the divorce. Try and forget you were ever married. The apartment's beautiful with 15-foot ceilings and hardwood floors and a totally renovated kitchen, but again one bedroom. Contemplate doing Pilates, yoga or weight training. You're forty-five and perimenopausal, you need to do it. *Fuck it.* You lift your aching bones off the bed. 6:45a.m. Put away sheets, covers. Make coffee. Put the cereal box on the table, maybe a couple of bananas and a pint of milk. Yes, you all still drink cow's milk even though it's probably causing cancer and acne and IBS. You are from West Virginia after all. Raised on biscuits. Wake kids up at 7:30a.m. Enough time to hustle out by 8:15a.m. The thirteen and four-year-old move as if slogging through slime. When you finally make it out of the apartment and onto Fort Washington, you avoid fighting with the prepubescent one. School is 0.6 miles away. You steer your four-year-old away from large piles of dog shit. Dodge cars, bicycles, scooters, strollers, people stumbling towards their next high on the steps of the church. Drop kids at 8:23a.m. exactly so that no one (said 13-year-old) has a nervous breakdown. Remember not to use the words crazy or bonkers or lunatic, even though you were raised in the 90's. Avoid having your own nervous breakdown as you remember that you forgot their water bottles and lunch and so they could dehydrate to death and will be forced to eat a wildly soggy or overly hard slice of pepperoni pizza, which is also definitely causing a listeria outbreak or cancer or disease or…pause. Check watch, phone, stoplight. Check your breath, heart rate, lung capacity, brain waves. 8:45a.m. Board the A train to 42nd street to West Side Studios. 18th floor. Rehearsal 10-1p.m. You only have enough money to reserve the space for three hours each day before you have to get to work to teach theater to kids. Warm up. *Unique New York. Unique New York. You know you need Unique New York. Red leather, yellow leather. The lips, the teeth, the tip of the tongue.* Stretch, bend, dance, run, laugh, wheel, wild. Remember you trained your whole life for this. Remember it matters. Theatre. Art. The truth. Remember why you wrote the show in the first place.

End rehearsal late and rush to the D train. Crowded now. Packed. People sleeping and drooling. Migrant mothers with babies strapped to their backs selling candy bars and chiclets. People hustled tight together. Stalled. Delayed. Cops with shoulders crossed. Cops eating donuts. Cliché after cliché. You fall asleep at 125th street and your neighbor jostles you awake at 167th. Bound out of the train and race to the corner of 165th and Washington Avenue. 15 minutes door-to-door if you run. Shin splints, aching ankles. Did you forget you are forty-five now? Slow down. You make it in twenty-three minutes. *You're late again,* the supervisor tells you. Apologize profusely. Tell her the train was stalled. Delayed. Your after-school theatre kids show up. 3p.m. They are rowdy, ready and hungry. They are teen-aged and drama and soda filled. They don't care what you look like. They care about trust. About honesty. They somehow seem to care less and less about social media. You trust these kids most of all. Twenty total. They show up every week. Three days a week to make devised theatre. You get to it. 5:30p.m. Run out to the D train again. Twenty-seven minutes this time. You are lagging. You are getting older every minute. Reframe. You are aging beautifully. You are spectacular. You are not sure that positive thinking actually works. But you are trying. Make the D train by 6p.m. Take the D to 145. Walk up what feels like 1,247 stairs. Actually seventy-five. But still. Transfer to the A train that goes from 145th to 168th. Get out early to pick up one lamb gyro and two falafel plates from the Halal Guys. They know you by name. It's somewhat embarrassing but at least it's food from your people. Your mom would be proud. Ask for extra vegetables and even though that's mostly fried onions, convince yourself you've got your children's best interests at heart. Speed the seven blocks home. Your kids are sitting still in front of the television. Their faces a highlighted glow. *How long have they been home?* Check your watch. An hour, ninety minutes tops. You check closer. They are both showered. Nothing educational is on, but nothing horrifying either. You don't throw your hands up in despair or weep into the dark night sky. You call them to the table. And you smell their clean, wet hair and you hold both of their small bodies to your own and you know that life is just one disaster away from ending all the fucking time. But not tonight. You are all lucky enough to still be breathing. You all sit and share a meal together. Before you collapse and hope to god that you get to do it all again. Tomorrow.

* * *

Willa arrives early for the audition. The hallways flooded with actors preening and pouting in front of their phone cameras; a hip bone plastered here and a jut of collarbone there. Willa took three deep breaths, pretending that stretching didn't hurt her aging hips and rolled her shoulders back. She was gonna rock this audition. When they called her name, she was more than ready.

"Yes. My name is Willa. It's lovely to meet you."

"That's a unique name," the casting director looks at the two others looking down at their clipboards. They glance up briefly and then check the fuck out.

"My name is Chloe. This is Anna and Devon."

Willa nods a hello.

"Hi. Nice to meet you all. And yes, Willa is a family name. My mom is from West Virginia and Kentucky. A true Appalachian. She named me after her mama Winifred. Definitely different." The casting director makes eyes at the others and smiles to herself.

"Well, could you go ahead and stand in front of camera number one and tell us a little bit about yourself?"

Willa needed this role. It was a part in a sitcom. What's the call exactly: sexy middle-aged mother? Stoic grandmother? The money would be steady. Theatre could be good for reputation, but not for the retirement account. At each audition, Willa felt like there were still doors that could open. They were on the 35th floor. She looked out at the whole of Manhattan, in all its complicated chaotic beauty, spread wide before her. A city she'd been traversing for the last several weeks trying to find "the best" public high school for her kid. She eyeballed the private schools along both the upper west and east sides, gave them a silent middle finger. She could even see all the way uptown toward Washington Heights and Inwood—her home; the place she felt most secure, even if that's not what her ex-husband Bryan envisioned for his first two kids. She never should have married a Bryan with a Y.

She took a breath in and looked at Chloe, Anna, and Devon. Congratulated herself for remembering their names.

"My name is Willa Harris, and I'm originally from West Virginia, but have been living in New York City—Washington Heights to be exact, for the last 25 years. My roots are from Assyria, Ireland, and Italy. My mom is Middle Eastern, maybe you can tell? I mean, I know I look White but I consider myself mixed-race and that complicates the way I see the world and the way it sees me."

She doesn't look up because she has said these words before.

"Let's see… I'm a former waitress and hostess, current teaching artist with several nonprofit arts in education programs and teach a couple of adjunct theatre classes at City College and am currently working on a project about school choice…" Willa hears a sharp sucking in of breath. She pauses, looks up, and at this moment, all eyes are on her.

"School choice?" Devon asks. He puts his clipboard down and looks directly at Willa. "For colleges or…"

"Oh, no. I am working on a solo show about school choice for kids who live in the city applying to public schools because that system is… basically fucked. I…have a soon to be 9th grader and a soon to be kindergartener, and I've been interviewing other families who like me are in this race to figure out the best options and frankly I'm wore out."

That's what her granny used to say, and suddenly she wished she could sit out of this race and go home. Just for a spell. She longed for the quiet. But there were no off-off Broadway stages, no auditions for sitcom pilots or national commercials, no snake-lines of actors waiting for their big break in West Virginia. Just massive mountains, winding country roads, gas stations stocked with beef jerky and homemade biscuits. Goddammit. She missed those biscuits.

Willa realizes they asked her to tell them about herself and she forgot she was auditioning for a role. But she didn't care. She wanted them to know who she wanted to be in the world. They either took it, or they didn't. They either wanted to know more, or they'd send her away with a thank you.

They all stare back at her now. Fully rapt. At attention. Focused. Clear.

"Oh my god!" Anna says. "We have a soon to be four-year-old. I hear you, loud and clear. Applying to school is so messed up, made to keep so many of our children out."

Devon looks at her, and Willa can see him grab Anna's hand quietly under the table.

"What?" Anna sneers at Devon. "We've been arguing about what is the best fit for our four-year-old. It's totally absurd but it's real."

Willa nods.

"Thank goodness, I don't have kids," Chloe adds, looks at the clock on the wall and is ready to continue with the audition.

"We live in Brooklyn, and it all depends on where the lines are drawn if your kid is zoned or not or gonna get into the specialized school or the art specific school or the fancy Oak Street Nursery program which is a pipeline for the even fancier Friends Academy which only does early family interviews with the Oak Street Nursery families..."

Anna looks at Willa as if she has the answers. She does not.

"Don't you want the best for your kids?" Devon asks. Clearly this is something that he and Anna have been arguing about. And Willa understood that she may have blown the audition but was getting some really good material for her solo show. She had been looking for more from the point of view of elite Brooklynites.

"I want the best for all kids," Willa said. "I don't want the best for my kids if it means the worst for your kids. But some people only think of their own kids."

Nobody says anything so she continues. "Family interviews, standardized tests, portfolios and admissions tests all have to do with proving you're better than someone else. And it's not just schools. It's housing and red lining and determining where people live and where they pay taxes and how their kids are schooled and by who and the demographics of who is included and who's not. That's the whole reason the 'Ivy League' exists. Whose Ivy League? What does that even mean?"

"Come on," Devon says suddenly, looking right at Willa now. "You can't be serious. I went to Brown. It's called the Ivy League for a reason."

"What's the reason?" Anna asks.

"They're top-ranking institutions around the world, Anna. You're talking highly competitive academics, world class sports, a rich history of elite…"

"That's it! Elite. I don't want our daughter to be pressured at four years old to be part of some elite bullshit cohort that exists to make others feel like shit."

Willa nods. If only she could take her phone out and start recording this conversation.

"You think going to NYU gave you a leg up," Anna says, looking at Chloe, and you," she keeps on, eyes on Devon now, "you think that going to Brown gave you a leg up? I went to SUNY Purchase. A state school, where I got enough scholarships and got out almost debt free and look at the three of us. Sitting here doing the same exact job. Right?" Chloe and Devon nod in agreement. "So, who is the sucker in this situation?"

"According to the world…it's you. Since you don't have a bumper sticker or a shirt or a tote bag that says *Ivy League for Life* or *Ivy League or Bust*. Right?" Willa says.

Willa starts to laugh a little. She's definitely not getting this job. She knows it. Maybe she lost the gig with her name or all the school choice talk or maybe it's when they realized she was an actual forty-five-year-old woman with two kids and not one that still looked thirty…no, twenty-seven. Often she was the only one with wrinkles or strands of gray hair. An anomaly in the business. A total freak show eventually. But still, she held onto the hope that women would eventually be able to grow older on camera. She wanted to look in the mirror and see a body and a face that had been through something. She wanted a face that could rage and weep. One that could be radical in its love and twisted with its fury. Complicated and ugly. She wanted to be able to be fucking ugly and not give a shit about fillers or Botox or things that puffed you up or exploded you or thinned you down or whatever the hell it was supposed to do to fix you. She did not want to be fixed after all. And she wanted to be someone who told the truth when it mattered and when it didn't. Just someone who showed up and said what needed to be said. Most of all, she wanted to have an opinion.

"We should really get started," Chloe says, smiling just slightly as if she was already trying not to damage her face with too much expression.

Take one – Hello my name is Willa Harris.

Say A Lil Prayer

Leo Martinez

Juan Luis was desperate. He ran to his mother's altar and dropped to his knees. A life-size statue of Our Lady of Mercy draped in a shawl of white gold held out her arms to receive him. He removed his cap and cowered in his lap. Outside, the rooster sang praises to the sun as the dawn mist faded on his father's farm; swords of light pierced through the window and refracted a yellow hue on his back.

"Please, please, please send Pablo back to me."

Tears fell to the floor.

"I'm not at peace; I can't sleep, can't eat. This love I feel for him… I've never felt for anyone. I want to give him a piece of my soul a-and spend my life forever with him. Please send Pablo back to me!"

Under the veil where you cannot see, a prayer materialized on the Lady's open palm and fell like a chinola from its tree. Dust-sized and glowing dimly, the prayer rolled back and forth. They had been preparing for their first mission to serve a greater good, but the prayer now lacked the will to move. They only knew that they had to find a "Pablo." What made them so important?

An elder spirit mounted Juan Luis to speak through him. An aura like the Lady raised above his body. His arms twisted and knocked over one of the glasses. Water doused the prayer, pushing them towards the doorway. The elder instructed the prayer:

Go to where the source of life smooths rocks,
Where love springs from dry ground,
Where you will find Pablo.
Pablo and Juan Luis' love has been ordained holy,
But human ignorance threatens them apart.
Do not verge off.
Do not take any detours.
Do not attempt to help anything else.
For you are their only hope.

The prayer gained more confidence, a new light. They stood upright and recalled needing large vessels to travel long distances. At that moment, the farm dog stepped into the altar room, curious to learn who was speaking so strange. The prayer climbed on his paw, and when the dog used it to scratch his head, they clung behind his ear like a flea.

The elder spirit returned under the veil, and Juan Luis remembered who he was. He heard a ringing in his ear and turned his head to the dog. For a moment, it was like he could see the prayer. The dog couldn't handle his intense look and skirted into the kitchen. Juan Luis turned back to the Lady's open arms.

* * *

Smelling the scent of stewed hen, the dog encountered Juan Luis's mother, who snatched the broom and smacked it on the floor. Her

"No, you dirty son of a bitch!" hurt the dog's feelings. He rushed out the front door and head-butted into a rooster, his black-blue comb wobbling. The dog yelped while the rooster got ready to fight. The prayer saw another opportunity and leaped to the rooster's wing. The rush of oxygen from the impact reminded the dog of his lover, the other male dog across the road. He ran to be with him to love on him unashamedly.

The rooster didn't know what to do with himself. He sang his morning song to celebrate that the sun had returned. What was he to do now? He scratched the red dirt, and his second purpose came to mind: fuck as much as he could in a single day.

The prayer, cocooned inside the rooster, gained more mass. They liked feeling heavy. Back home, they were massless, but Juan Luis's words became their flesh. Here, they weren't just one of many. They don't have to submit to the collective will or consider the greater good; they could be selfish. They had heard so much about this world's strange creatures with too much knowledge. Humans were known to enslave, eat, and bury alive their own kind, yet they were still worthy of our mercy?

Then they remembered what their elders had chanted to their students: Everything here dissolves into chaos. If you are lost there, then you can never return. No, they had a mission and didn't want to spend one more minute here than necessary.

While the prayer contemplated their free will, the rooster made his way to the hen house, and the girls weren't having it. He clucked around them, waving his comb and puffing up his chest, but they ignored him. He called out their names; they side-eyed him and chuckled at his clownery.

Tired of the rooster's games, the prayer needed a new vessel. They peeked out of the wings and looked at the environment: bored hens, a tree with too many mangoes, cows napping under the shade of that tree, hills and more hills, and beyond that, more hills—nothing was moving anytime soon. They sulked inside the wing's darkness; would they remain in this realm forever?

A bell rang. Confused, the prayer saw a yellow cow pushing against the wired fence.

"That farmer's always too damn drunk to take care of us," she yelled, "and his kids sit on their asses! I don't get any fresh water! Fuck this shit; I'm going to the river!"

The river—where love springs from dry ground! She was their opportunity! They fled from the rooster at the right moment because he, not caring that the hens weren't interested, forced himself on the slowest one to run.

Hopping to the cow was challenging: patches of morirvivis littered the ground, and its green leaves shut at the prayer's presence. Morirvivis were said to fear being uprooted.

The prayer bounced from stalk to stalk to avoid danger. Cut by the wire, the cow wailed, and caught off guard, the prayer slammed into the plant's softness. They struggled to free themself. The leaves smothered them, tiring them out. They could imagine spending the rest of their existence there when they laid down on its soft fibers. The plant, sure of its safety, opened again. The prayer saw the cow halfway through the fence, her body scraping against the now bloody wires. Bouncing on the red-orange dirt, they hooked themselves onto her tail, the last part of her body to escape.

* * *

Juan Luis's father woke up hungover that afternoon and went to the window to see his property: his wife scrubbing the patio floor, his rooster harassing the hens, his cows getting fatter. He noticed a lack of color among the cows and was pissed to find his yellow cow had escaped. A buyer who wanted to breed her and sell her offspring planned to pick her up later that day.

The farmer cussed out his wife for her negligence. She came up to him and shifted the guilt to him. "Don't disrespect me, stupid. You know I don't give two shits about those cows. They shit everywhere! You told the boys to watch her—remember, asshole? And you smell like shit. Go wash your ass, and I'll get your food."

The farmer wanted to smack her smart mouth but needed to leave. He grumbled to himself and washed his face, armpits, and ass crack.

He called his sons to the kitchen. Most of his children—all boys, no girls—left the farm to work in the city because that's where the money flowed. They were dead to the farmer. His family came from a long line of men who farmed back when their ancestors were forced to work on someone else's land. Now they own their own land; how could they leave behind their overdue reparations? Those who remained were his youngest: twenty-something Juan Luis and his pre-teen twins.

He spat curses at their faces while he ate stewed hen with mashed auyama. Juan Luis, hoping to appease him, said, "I was praying at Mami's shrine, Pa. And I sent the twins to buy some casabe."

The farmer narrowed his eyes and grabbed Juan Luis's ear. Twisting it clockwise, he said God was not going to rain money. If he wanted to pray, the farmer suggested he chop off his dick and join a monastery. The twins stayed quiet to avoid their father's wrath.

When his anger plateaued, he announced that they were catching that cow. Juan Luis heard something ringing in his ear again. The twins started up their shared motorbikes; the farmer got on Juan Luis's bike, rubbing Juan Luis's head like he'd done when he was a baby.

They all rode through the gate; his wife, hands on her lower back, asked God, "When will this life get easier?"

* * *

Licking the snot from her nose, the cow trotted down the road. The prayer moved up to her head for a better view than her ass; they rested near her ear and processed all the emotions they had experienced: greed, anger, desire, despair. This was what humans experience daily? Back home, everything could behave as one being, one consciousness. But here, humans cause problems for themselves and scatter.

The cow slowed to eat a patch of tall weeds. She closed her eyes and chewed on its fresh bitterness. It tasted like the first time she could eat all by herself without the milk of her mama, who was sold to another farmer and never seen again. A cruelty the cow never forgave, she held onto her pain and turned her rage into hating her master, his family, and all humans.

As she moved forward, she bumped into a charred body hidden in the grass. Its head, hands, and genitals were cut off. The parts that weren't burned to a crisp were black-blue bruised.

"A-ha!" she laughed, seeing the truth that humans could be ruthless with each other. The prayer, on the other hand, was sympathetic. They knew that a desecrated person's soul could never sleep in peace. These kinds of souls stuck between the veil and here would complain about every pain they could remember. No one listens to them. How could they transition when their histories were erased? Maybe living in this realm was not easy.

The cow ate around the body until it was visible. She wanted other humans to see they could be slaughtered.

The cow marched forward while the prayer retreated into their fears. They had no clue what they were going to do. From their vantage point, they still saw fields and, beyond that, more fields. Where would they even find Pablo? He could be anywhere at any time. Why would the elders put them in a difficult situation like this? One part of them remained steadfast, but the prayer was scared.

* * *

Looking down at the river out of the window, Pablo considered jumping out and smashing his skull—his organs and blood splattered on the stone. No more love, no more passion, no more heartbreak. It was easier to imagine that than his present. It was a dissociation skill he learned from his mother, who learned from her mother, who learned from her mother, who saw her parents shot in the head by an American soldier.

When Death visited and took his father, Pablo's mother was no longer anchored in this realm. Unless she was working at the lottery post, she watched TV all day: telenovelas, poorly-dubbed Turkish movies, debates justifying a bigger border wall, anything that moved with saturated colors. When the electricity went out, she would light candles and read Psalms like her matriarchs had done.

Pablo was an only child, so he had to manage the house. Do the cleaning, cooking, and shopping. During his downtime, he would absently gaze at the river, waiting for a prince to save him, or the wood grain beneath him, conjuring shapes that told him stories of old hurt.

Five nights ago, Juan Luis visited Pablo's home for the first time.

"What kind of person wouldn't meet their friend's mother?" Pablo's mother, suspicious of where her son was going at night, needed to see Juan Luis; she was insistent. It was a rare moment of clarity that annoyed Pablo. As long as she had her TV and Bible, why would she care if he was gone for an hour or the whole night?

Juan Luis rode his bike across the bridge and parked the motorbike in Pablo's home. He heard the river's soothing sounds. It helped him feel a little more confident. Pablo came out and kissed him on the cheek.

After the necessary greetings, she sat them down on the couch. Out of respect, they left enough room for the Holy Spirit; Juan Luis tucked his cap between his knees. The electricity had gone out on time; lit candles cast tender shadows.

She asked, "I always see you picking up my Pablo almost every night. Where do you two go?"

Pablo's embarrassment heated his chest. Was she aware of what he was doing this whole time? They had been on the "down low" for over two years, understanding the unspoken rule that anything queer provokes violent reactions.

Juan Luis responded, "No, señora, we are just friends. We go to drink beers and have a good time, that's all."

"A good time, my ass. Pablo doesn't come back home till the rooster crows—I counted three times last week. What kind of friends you two are?" The shadow deepened the wrinkles surrounding her eyes.

Pablo's rebelliousness empowered him, saying *fuck it* to the pressure to be silent and said, "Yes, we're more–"

Juan Luis turned to face Pablo and shot him a *you-fucking-serious-right-now* look.

"No, of course not, we are friends, señora—that's it," Juan Luis corrected; he was not ready for this conversation. How could he be when he didn't tell his parents?

Pablo's mother sighed. "Listen, I know my son… more woman than man. I see no problem, but people can take advantage of that kind of softness."

"We only spend an hour or so together. I don't know who else he goes to see," Juan Luis half chuckled. Pablo's heart flinched.

"You calling my son dirty?"

"No, no, no—but I-I don't know what he does when I go home."

The Holy Spirit between them turned tense. Pablo lost touch with this reality for a moment; he instead focused on the flickering candlelight that wanted to go out.

"You two can go do—whatever you planned."

They stood up and walked out of the house. Pablo didn't want to be near Juan Luis, and Juan Luis's pride kept him from explaining his fear. Their love was brought to the burning light.

Juan Luis revved his bike's engine and left Pablo behind. Powerless to the deep-rooted shame that loomed like an eternity, Pablo decided it would be better to leave him alone and turned his back. The exhaust's smoke shrouded Juan Luis until he was just red lights on the road.

* * *

Seeing an unaccompanied yellow cow walk alone did turn some heads— more than a rotting body. The exploited farm hands with bundles of batatas on their backs were too tired to capture her. Besides, everyone in the town knew that taking another man's property led to gunfire. They would be the ones who later told the farmer and his sons where they had seen her and in which direction she was headed.

At a crossroads three miles from the river, an overseer, a good friend of the farmer, reined in his white horse to block the cow's path. He pulled out a lasso and threw and tightened it around her neck.

The prayer heard her gasping air and shrieking, "Let me go! Let me go!"

She twisted her head and stomped her hooves. Orange dust flew everywhere. The overseer used all his strength to restrain her irrational movements. Why wouldn't she obey the noose around her neck?

Her cries became desperate. "I can't go back, I can't go back, I don't want to disappear, I don't want to disappear! Help me, please, help me!"

The overseer laughed, feeling primal power rising in his chest as he watched her suffer. The prayer was paralyzed, powerless against this senseless cruelty. What could they do? If she was dragged back to the farm, they would be back where their journey started. Time wasted. They pleaded for a miracle—please let God be true quickly!

An ashy-faced owl swooped in. She clawed on the arm that held the lasso. The horse, shocked to see an owl during the day, stood on its hind legs. The overseer fell on his back! The owl flew to the fallen man and tormented him, her talons cutting deep into his skin. He had no choice but to run away, and his horse ran after him.

The owl flew to the nearest post to be eye-to-eye. "My sister, are you ok?"

"No, I'm not," her tone quivered, "I can't be at peace nowhere." The noose lingered like a bruise.

"Nowhere I can be at peace. Maybe leaving my farmer was a mistake."

The owl squinted at her. "You came from a farm?"

"Yeah, I was thirsty for fresh water—for something to nourish me. My spirit's weak, and I thought the water from the river can heal me, you know what I mean?"

She flapped her wings. "That will not happen, you know that? Your owner will be coming for you, and you will be put in the same place where you were. I see it all the time. I only helped you because your screams woke me. I am actually upset to be here in the first place—over some farm cow."

"I didn't ask you for your help. Get the fuck out!"

"Don't bite the claw that fed you, stupid cow. Be grateful that I got rid of that human. Go back before you are dragged back."

"You don't know shit about me or what I've been through, so don't tell me what I should do!"

The owl turned her back and flew away, leaving the cow to spiral: "Owls are supposed to be wise, and us cows mindless, right? What do I know? Do I know what I want? Why am I here—all these terrible decisions I made—what'll they do to me? Shit, shit, shit, I'm fucked." She couldn't move nor cry—her heart beating slower. The prayer trembled as they felt a darkness overtaking her. Crap, they didn't plan on caring about this cow; she was just a vessel to get to the river. In this situation, the elders would advise them to find another vessel.

No, the prayer couldn't do that; they understood the gravity of her pain: she had been mistreated, objectified, and attacked. Her life was not hers. Compassion sprouted inside the prayer and bore love. Forget about the mission! Their priority was to convince her to keep going to the river.

Moving inside her ear, they sat inside and hummed a soft chant they had learned long ago. The cow heard a ringing that wouldn't stop—a ringing that reverberated through her body, reaching her heart. In her mind, she heard:

Praise our mother of good that cools heads
Your water fills us
You who give babies to barren mothers
Praise our mother
You who gushes love from dry earth
Please help us flow like you

A hidden memory rushed to the front of the cow's mind: *When she was a calf, she, her mother, and the other cows were being herded through the mountains and had to cross the nearby river. The herd complained about getting wet, but her mother loved it. It was the first time the cow saw her mother laugh, her black and brown cowhide radiating. She splashed and played until the farmer whipped her. Her mother's light was strong at the river.*

The cow, excited to immerse herself in the water, lowered her head, stepped on the rope to free herself, and walked on.

The farmer and his sons caught up with the defeated overseer. He told them they weren't far from catching her and explained how he was attacked. The farmer pissed himself laughing. Imagine it—a strong man defeated by a cranky owl. The overseer looked unaffected but made a silent epiphany that he clung to for the rest of his life and would pass down to his children and their children: *God doesn't like ugly.*

* * *

Lifting his legs over the window's ledge, Pablo heard his neighbors drinking their extra-large beers and barbecuing freshly killed beef. Speakers from another century blasted songs about lovers' strife. He saw their kids run up the rocky hill to the colmado and come back with more beers and ice.

Pablo didn't like them—plain and simple—but for a good reason. Never once did they pick up after themselves, leaving all their trash on the bank. They technically weren't breaking any laws since the police spent their energy on protecting the rich landowners and harassing migrant workers from Haiti rather than caring about a little river.

He had confronted them two weeks ago, coming up in jean shorts and a cropped Tweety Bird t-shirt. That day, there were three couples; each girlfriend sat on their boyfriend's lap; one of the girls had the biggest, gnarliest mole above her upper lip.

"Hey, pick up your trash," he screamed over the speakers.

They laughed at his face. The girl with the hairy mole giggled, "What's this lil birdie saying?"

"I said, pick up your trash! The trash you leave here hurts the river. We wash our clothes here. We bathe here. We depend on it! You treat it like it's nothing!"

"Jaja! Clean it yourself; we know you're a good housemaid."

The girl threw a glass bottle in his direction. He flinched to avoid its shattering trajectory. Pablo had decided that it would be better to leave them alone than confront them.

Before deciding to take the plunge down, a familiar yellow cow walked over the bridge; Pablo couldn't believe it—that meant Juan Luis must be close by! They could talk and hold each other again. He scrambled to change his clothes into something sexy.

The men outside of the colmado made kissy noises at the cow, demanding her to give them her milk. She whipped her tail at them as she went down the hill. The cow felt the river's presence like she did as a calf. The couples, surprised to see this party crasher, sucked their teeth to get her attention. Their kids were more excited to see her and ran to stroke her. But the cow wasn't stopping for anybody. The malicious kids threw rocks. The prayer understood a fundamental truth of this realm: when you stood out, humans othered you.

A boy grabbed the end of her tail. She kicked him right in the chest, shattering his ribs, puncturing his lungs, collapsing his breath. The other kids yelled for the boy's mother, the girl with the hairy mole; when she approached him, her concern came out as curses: "God fucking damn it, this boy gone kill himself! You had be a fucking dumbass. I can't, just—"

A small crowd appeared on the bridge, and seemingly-concerned people shook their heads. The boy's father, almost thirty years older than his wife, pushed through the crowd to get his pickup truck. When he backed near the top of the hill, the men from the party picked up the boy and placed him gently on the truck's bed. He was coughing blood. His mother was still on the bank, crouched, crying, panicking. The honk of the truck startled her, but she knew it was time to go and ran to the passenger seat.

Disregarding the chaos, the cow sloshed into the water; its coolness calmed her nerves; its pebbles massaged her hooves; its silky mud healed her ankles. Far enough in, she bent down—her hind legs first and then her front—to sit down, be still, let the current curve over her. She submerged her mouth and drank the water; it tasted fresh. Eyes closed and ears tingling, she listened to the river whispering; the voice was clear.

Shhhwooshhhhhhhh, the river said.

The cow heard, *My child, I am here—you are safe.*

The prayer had leaped off the cow after she kicked that boy and climbed on top of a nearby boulder. The cow did not rejoice like they assumed, but she radiated peace. Exhausted and not knowing where to go to complete the mission, they slowed down and entered a meditative space. Would the elders punish them for not following their orders and banish them here? Who cares—getting the cow here mattered more. They rested and trusted that God would show them a way to return home.

* * *

At the height of the panic, Juan Luis, leading his family, arrived on the other side of the bridge. He beeped his horn, but the crowd wasn't moving. He parked his bike, and his brothers did the same. The farmer yelled what the hell was going on, and an older woman who heard replied, "A poor woman got her heart stomped on by a horse!"

"Ma, what?" her middle-aged daughter turned to the farmer, "A boy got kicked in the chest by that yellow cow. Ma, who told you that lie? I swear, you look so stupid talking shit!"

The farmer didn't have the time to entertain their bickering and plunged into the crowd. The twins followed, but Juan Luis detoured. Pablo had to be nearby. They had to talk; he missed holding the person he cared for most in this world.

Pablo, dressed in a golden tank top and green capris, felt Juan Luis's energy and rushed to find him. He was no longer in control of his body; a ringing in his ear filled his heart.

Just as the truck carrying the injured boy and weeping mother got on the road, it almost swerved into the farmer. Releasing the pent-up anger about his life, his shitty job, and the futility of leaving behind generations of poverty, he kicked the door on the driver's side and left a huge dent. He messed with the wrong person that day. The father put the emergency brakes on and leaped out, leaving the truck perched on top of the hill. He grabbed the farmer's neck and slammed him to the ground.

"Get back in the car!" the mother cried.

The twins rushed to save their father and sneaked in a few punches at him, then men from the party came to support their friend, then men who believed the farmer was an innocent bystander came to help him. The men who wanted to break up this brawl came too, and then their women ran to pull their loved ones before they broke their necks.

The mother screamed, "This's fucking ridiculous—put your pride away! Stop this nonsense!"

The crowd swarmed with more people and intensity, hard to tell what was a cry or cheer. Pablo, smushed between a bickering mother and daughter, wanted to give up and shut down. Was it delusional to think Juan Luis would be here?

Juan Luis jumped over a bleeding man and landed on a fire ant hill. The queen ant alerted her soldiers that they were under attack. The fire ant squadron swarmed Juan Luis's ankle. He yelled in pain; Pablo recognized that scream. He listened, his pulse slowing. His yells reverberated into Pablo's eardrums. He turned to the right, where Juan Luis struggled to release himself. Pablo charged towards him. Juan Luis grabbed Pablo's hand; gripping Pablo's knuckles, Juan Luis flew into Pablo's arm. Like a star exploding, the impact blasted a passion so great that the prayer heard the lingering ring it created.

They looked at each other and couldn't speak. Apologies and bitterness filled their throats, but love beamed through their hearts. They sneaked behind the colmado to reconcile privately.

The boy's mother was not going to let her son die. She got into the driver's seat, clutching the stick, and tried to put it into drive. It stopped in neutral.

"This shit won't let me go!" She shook the stick while the truck shook with the men outside fighting. The dashboard blinked that the emergency brakes were set. She reached under, stretched her left leg, and released it. Right before she could grab the stick, the boy's father was pushed hard against the rear bumper; the truck rolled down the hill too fast to comprehend.

Everyone stopped.

They all ran down, falling over each other like stones in an earthquake.

Struggling to balance herself, the mother was too stunned to act; a memory of when her mother had lost control of the car and almost plummeted down a steep hill hit her body. Like she did that day, she jumped out. The boulders caught her, but the bones in her back snapped. Half of the crowd, led by the farmer, went to rescue the mother, and the other half, led by the father, followed the truck.

The truck rushed past the boulder the prayer was on and headed for the river. The water softened the crash and soaked the boy. The sudden cool water pushed Death's hand away from the boy's throat.

The splash alerted the cow that she wasn't alone. She opened her eyes, and, for a moment, she and the farmer held each other's gaze.

"I'm not going back," she said to herself. She started to run until her hoovers couldn't touch the sediment. The water caught her and shielded her body; she became a part of the river.

The farmer couldn't help but cry, moving aside to let the other men help the mother.

The boy was still breathing, but his skin turned pale. The father got inside the truck and put it into drive. The men who had beaten the crap out of each other were now ramming their bodies against the truck to push it out of the river. The truck flew out and landed on the rocks, annoyed to sustain the enormous weight. The father stopped at the bottom of the hill so that they could place the mother in the truck beside her child. The hurt from abandoning her child, worse than her broken bones, calmed when she cradled his head and felt his breath as the truck dashed off.

* * *

Juan Luis, on his knees, felt the rapture he experienced at the shrine, but he choked on his words. Opening his heart tightened his throat. Also on his knees, Pablo held his lover's hands and initiated the conversation: "I know we haven't talked since that night… I've missed you."

"I-I've missed you so much," Juan Luis said, taking off his cap and casting his eyes on the red dirt. "I don't like it when we're fighting."

"Me neither…." A breath before he asked: "Were you afraid of my mom knowing about us?"

Juan Luis's gut clenched, and he squeezed Pablo's hands. "You know you remember when I first said 'I love you' here?"

The memory hit their bodies before their minds could remember: *On the holiday of Our Lady of Mercy and the anniversary of his father's passing, Pablo had drunk too much white rum and decided that he needed to swim in the river. Juan Luis was against it since Pablo was bumbling, but Pablo got his way, batting his dark-brown eyes and long lashes that Juan Luis could get lost looking into. By the river bank, Pablo undressed down to his underwear, unleashing the gravity of his wide hips, and Juan Luis couldn't help but feel a pull in his jeans.*

"Take off your clothes and come in with me, baby," Pablo slurred.

"Someone has to be dry just in case," Juan Luis laughed.

Arms spread out for balance, Pablo walked into the water, and he looked behind and saw Juan Luis looking like an archangel. He reached in and splashed some water on his head and chest; the tingling on his nipples tickled him. He splashed more water on himself; the drops sparkled like jewels not of this world.

"Come closer, baby, the water's cool, baby."

"I'm fine where I'm at."

"I guess I need to bring the water to you," Pablo squealed before rushing to where Juan Luis stood, but before he could soak him, his feet stepped on a too-slippery rock, and he fell on his ass. Juan Luis laughed not because Pablo was in pain but because the first words Pablo screamed were, "Juan Luis, help me!"

He picked up Pablo in his arms, feeling the rush when their skins touched, and kissed his forehead. Pablo whimpered that he wanted to go home.

"Ok, baby, let me take you home."

"No! Not to my mom! I want to go home with you—have you by my side."

The bold assertion caused Juan Luis to stop moving. "No... not today—but we'll have a home together, I promise, we will."

Pablo sucked his teeth. "I get so lonely without you."

"We will have a home together."

"You don't mean that; you lie, lie, I—"

"No, I will never lie to you—Pablo, I love you."

Stunned to hear the words he longed to hear, Pablo remained quiet as Juan Luis helped him dress again; the river purred in the background.

"I told you the truth in my heart."

Pablo almost cried, reliving the moment, and smiled. "Yes, I remember—you carried me back home after I busted my ass."

The memory's warmth evaporated their anxieties. "You know, I'll always, always love you, Pablo, that's never going to change, b-but—"

"And I will always love you… and we don't need people to know our business, right?"

Between them, the question lingered: will their love always be hidden?

* * *

It was quiet after the truck left; everyone went back home to begin their nightly rituals. The townspeople laughed that something had possessed them. Wives and daughters cooked dinner while the men cleaned their wounds and gossiped about who was the weakest during the brawl.

Juan Luis and Pablo, holding hands, ran into the farmer, wailing by the bridge. The twins were ready to go home, annoyed that their father was crying like a baby. Juan Luis's fear spiked in his heart like it had that awful night, but holding Pablo's hand reminded him of what he had almost lost.

The prayer, deep in meditation, hummed the chant to the river they had done earlier as Juan Luis charged to them and pulled Pablo behind him.

"Pa, I know that it's not a good time, but… this is Pablo, and, and—"

Juan took off his cap, inhaling to quiet the ringing in his head, "I've been leaving the farm to see him almost every night 'cause—"A squeeze from Pablo's hand jolted Juan Luis to say what had been unspeakable. "—we're together. I—I love him, Pa, and he loves me."

"Nice to meet you, señor!" Pablo blurted.

The farmer's tears stopped flowing like he had been slapped. Worried about how he would afford to maintain his farm, he couldn't process the fact that his son was a faggot. That day, he lost another son to that city lifestyle. His blank expression concealed how repulsed he was. He nodded indifferently at Pablo and said it was about time for him and the twins to head home. The farmer and the twins squeezed onto one seat, leaving the other motorbike behind; the truth was that the farmer didn't want to ride with Juan Luis, a stranger to him.

"Well—that went like I feared it would…." Juan Luis placed his cap back on, his voice cracking.

"Listen, I'm here by your side—you're not alone, ok?"

Juan Luis smiled and kissed Pablo's forehead.

On a weary high after the hot-air shame had released its pressure, they stayed at the bank to talk about a new future they could build together—imagined collecting moonlight, dew drops, fluffy clouds, and smooth crystals to make the home where they could be at peace.

Rested, the prayer became aware of their surroundings. They climbed down the boulder and caught Juan Luis holding onto someone. Walking towards them, they heard him say,

"Christ, Pablo, if you think about it, if that cow didn't come here—"

It was Pablo! The elders were wrong; the detour, the divergence, helping the cow was God's way! Then they noticed that the cow was gone; the spot she sat now shrouded in a shadow. They hoped she was at peace.

The couple stayed out until the stars blossomed in the sky.

Lying on Juan Luis' chest, Pablo asked, "Can you take me back to my mom's?"

"As long as I can come in."

Pablo blushed. "Yeah, that shouldn't be a problem."

Their mission now completed, the prayer decided to remain at the river, the only place that reminded them of how their home under the veil felt.

Juan Luis turned on the bike, and Pablo held on to his waist tight. The waning moon lighted their way. Passing them on the road was the truck from earlier, with Death following right behind.

Juan Luis slowed down when something large approached them. He turned on the headlights and saw the cow, drenched in water but alive. She was shocked to see the farmer's son, but he was smiling. He didn't try to capture or stop her. She hurried into the bush.

"If she wants to be free so bad, then she better survive," Juan Luis laughed.

In front of Pablo's house, Juan Luis turned off the engine and sighed. They could see the TV's blue light and his mother's flickering shadow.

"Come inside," Pablo said, nudging into Juan Luis's neck, "We can talk with her again. Remember, I'm here by your side, ok?" He kissed Juan Luis, who thanked God for answering his prayer. Later that night, cracking up at Juan Luis's jokes about the huge brawl, Pablo's mother felt like she gained another son.

* * *

Back at the river, the veil lifted, and the prayer could see the golden darkness where they came from. They hesitated to go; once they go through, it could be decades or centuries before they are called to come back. The bridge would be destroyed. This town would be gone. The people they saw would be dead. Everything man-made will be changed. But this river would still be here; maybe she would remember what happened today.

The prayer returned where you cannot see.

Schlegel's Fragments

Anna Kreienberg

This is what my erotomania has done to me. It has made my life the dreams of a delirious sick person or an unfinishable letter to you—one I cannot even start because I am so caught on my view out the window. And yet—despite the fact that I do not know what to say to you or about myself—my life is richer than ever. This crush has unspooled imagination in the most exciting ways. I am giving myself nodes preparing a Sharon Van Etten impression, just for the pleasure of it. I am reading Lyn Hejinian and it is making sense. I am having the most amazing dreams. In one of them, I am introduced to Megan Thee Stallion at a bar. We hit it off immediately. When the conversation comes to a natural pause, she remarks she has enjoyed the evening and calls me "dashing." Dashing! I wake myself up smiling.

* * *

But how to construct a text to a woman in such an epistolary era as ours?

"In some ways, I know deep down I'm straight by the fact I want a phalloplasty to be able to fuck you. And maybe if I write my feelings into something just a bit longer, I may be able to win a Lambda or some literary money in order to get it"

I clear the message body. It was Schlegel who wrote that "Nothing is more contemptible than sorry wit." I really find him so inspiring.

I draft and delete: "Don't you think solar eclipse glasses are an experiment by big ophthalmology?"

The science of eyes, of sight. Looking out into the bright-darkness of the covered sun, receiving what I am imagining is a Lasik vivisection—which is a thought I'd like to share with you, although I'm not sure it's sufficiently witty yet, and so I let it be—I ideate. Perhaps a kind of Junie B. Jones-style message? and I think about a message that might comment best on the state of the world, the eclipse a kind of commentary for all these earthly discourses, these pieces of leather that form the sick bit upon which I chomp. Even though me and my coworkers' perceptual apparatuses are all being phenomenally expanded to the point of total clarity, even if we are uniquely placed to have some insights into the heavens, we are still all thinking about the human condition, I imagine. Our hovels, even. Except I am actually thinking about the feminine condition, and that I do not care at all that we are under the same gray sun, our pupils turning into the heads of pins, transmuting like those of curious goats. I don't find it romantic at all. Perhaps I should write what I see.

* * *

The eclipse's surround. An eerie quality of light, the premature dimming of the day's stage. Driving home from the college where I work as a secretary, I see young people looking directly at the sun. Some fearlessly, nakedly exposing their eyes—that unique nervous organ—bare to the sky. I find myself inside instead of out, feeling that perhaps regular estrangement from nature is not so bad if we get to have these special moments of oracular and anticipatory blindness, together.

* * *

Driving gives me time to come up with the perfect messages.

"How was your day in the symbiotic morass?"

"Short story idea: woman who gets extremely horny reading Lacan"

"Schlegel said that 'sapphic poems must grow and be discovered'—what do you think? also, 'grow' before 'discovered'? order seems off right?"

I hit the curb really hard and turn off a crime podcast. After parking, I walk towards home.

* * *

Schlegel: "Women are treated as unjustly in poetry as in life. If they're feminine, they're not ideal, and if ideal, not feminine."

* * *

At home, I talk to my neighbors on the porch. A bit about the weather, the pesticides I put in a bucket in the backyard for the mosquitos, the fact that the landlord is selling the house. The color of the sky does not inspire more description, although the coloring is suggestive of something odd in its history, reminiscent of the wildfire smoke that had settled the air quality earlier last year.

In the place of the political and structural discourses that had dominated the issue previously, a new form of respiratory orthorexia traveled in on the breeze. People were buying air purifiers and wearing masks. They were taking off work and staying inside. Back then, an ex called and asked if he should be concerned about moving down the street from some kind of waste dump in Brooklyn, something we would have never thought twice about until we heard all of this constant horrible stuff about the air. We both perversely tried to take some comfort in the fact that there is an elementary school even closer to the dump than the apartment at hand. I think, deep down, I just did not want this to be a problem. I encouraged him to at least see the place and then I smoked a cigarette outside, knowing that the disease I could get from this particular one was intensified by the blazing, the killer wind.

* * *

Michèle Montrelay: "I never say to myself: 'I am writing as a woman, I am going to get this message across better than a man, or not as well.' What is important, I repeat, is the unconscious."

* * *

I like how they translate Marx, how they make him say that it is the "sensual" or "sensuous" world. It is not impossible to imagine Marianne Williamson saying the same thing, for example. That's an appreciable vulgarity. And there is something erotic to the world as it is perverted for the purposes of information, and even to the way that information might be transmitted. To stay merely in the moment to moment of embodied experience, in all its temporariness and solitude, is dull and disordering. It disappoints. It's why the genre of poems about plucking out one's pussy hairs, written in English but with the air of translation from the French, has been a major contributor to cultural mortification. But to lend one's sensuous black box to language, this might be worth going on for.

* * *

Walter Pater: "The service of philosophy... towards the human spirit, is to rouse, to startle it into sharp and eager observation. Every moment some form grows perfect in hand or face; some tone on the hills or the sea is choicer than the rest; some mood of passion or insight or intellectual excitement is irresistibly real and attractive for us,—for that moment only. Not the fruit of experience, but experience itself, is the end."

* * *

What would it even mean to write a text like that, one that could rouse or startle a woman? I pace, I percolate. Should I tell her about how I recently saw *The Texas Chainsaw Massacre,* and have been admiring the way it alchemizes the shrill laughter of desiring, beautiful women, transfiguring it into shrieks at the edge of death? That's what I would like to tell her about, but there is such a thing as too startling. It's not about the fruit of experience.

* * *

Of course it's impossible to be fully in the sensuous world. One hears about people who get too far into spirituality courses and celibacy and begin seeing things for what they really are all the time. It is the veil between real life and sense data that keeps us observing. If one gains direct access, they also lose observation—a loss that occurs in the real.

* * *

I walk inside and sit down at the kitchen table to think. But there is only so much desecration I can take.

At the very moment of fantasizing about the various ways my continued desecration would manifest, NPR begins the assault: a segment about how young people are using generative AI to write each other love letters. When the radio broadcasts your thoughts—this is the exact kind of psycho-structural vulnerability that love creates, the kind that threatens observation. Well it's a good thing I am being defensively mindful. My kitchen knick-knacks are in perfect order. The little cats are swarming the surfaces, all of the devices and lights are humming in complementary frequencies, and my sweatshirt snugs correctly and where it should, at the wrists and neck. These evidence my observational abilities are intact—the veil sheathes, relieves the real of oversaturated potential meanings.

But the cosmological thoughts are still beckoning—the magical thinking creates a salaciousness where before there was nothing. God destined the creation and sending of this text message. God created this NPR broadcast, and God affirms my adoration by adorning it with a brilliant (but still, secondary) goal—to stop AI with the power of letters.

* * *

Lots of people want to stop AI with letters. I recently attended an academic conference where many people talked about what might be good about AI, what we might be able to steal back from the machines. After yet another talk about its possible usefulness, an audience member quietly pushed back on the entire weekend's perseverations. Straining, she named the dangers of the proposed AI collusion. She spoke about the environmental devastation that was looking us right in the face, that we were literally producing. She described how we had a unique opportunity, at this juncture in time, to really actually do something. To stand up and say no.

AI is a hot, demanding object—it is a tenement of dry wires connecting devices, a mechanical bricolage more like Aronofsky's *Pi* than Gilliam's *Brazil*. It needs a septic sip of the pesticide bucket. It needs to belch gas into the sunless sky.

The protestor in the crowd invokes Schlegel, who writes "Like animals, the spirit can only breathe in an atmosphere made up of pure life-giving oxygen mixed with nitrogen. To be unable to tolerate and understand this fact is the essence of foolishness; to simply not want to do so, is the beginning of madness."

* * *

The German critic and philosopher Schlegel is described as a cunty child who became a genius and died a proselytizing tradcath. He is saintly in this way—how real that kind of trajectory is, how honestly reactionary to one's own developmental movements. Other people did not like him because he was very annoying. He writes, for example, "You are not really supposed to understand me, but I want very much for you to listen to me." He hardly ever finished any of his writing projects. Even his lauded fragments—that mega-pith of notes, musings, and reviews scraped from notebooks over years—were (supposedly) ultimately intended to constellate a solar system of literature, and give better shape to all of literary thought. To prepare us to apprehend the word. Each fragment, he wrote, must be a "miniature work of art," and had to "be complete in itself like a porcupine."

He was too needling, his thoughts too spikey to generate a total theory of everything. Schlegel's fragments are authoritative. Naturally, he is a hater. This is kind of funny, because most every reader and critic—among them Kierkegaard, even—despised his novel, *Lucinde: Confessions of a Blunderer.* Semi-autobiographical, horny, preachy, and of course—unfinished—it is considered a truly terrible book in most respects. It begins with a lover's letter to his sweetheart. At first, he excites himself with the promise of sharing his history—sharing of his very self—with his desired object. He goes on, glowing in anticipation of then producing a radiant account of the couple's shared life. But he makes some insane detours. First, he gets distracted from his task by looking out the window. Then, he discloses that even though he has been writing prolifically, he basically messed up the order of the pages so badly that he is just going to present all of this testimony as "dreams." He is just going to do the best he can. The protagonist is thus forced to claim an "incontestable right to confusion"—and he transforms his executive function problems into an intervention on genre. He promises to disorder the novel, to give it an arrhythmia. Only this way can he accomplish the real task of writing—to collect and record that observational data necessary for the elaboration of "the loveliest situation in this most beautiful world."

* * *

It does not seem that people are finding women's private philosophical notebooks. Or perhaps they are just being published as different genres.

* * *

Schlegel loved Diderot, who loved Sophie Volland. In a letter to Volland, Diderot writes: "Look at the circuitous paths we have taken. The dreams of a delirious sick person are not any more heteroclite.

And yet, just as nothing is disconnected in the head of a dreamer or a madman, everything holds tighter likewise in conversations, but sometimes it would be quite difficult to reconstruct the imperceptible links that held so many disparate ideas together."

* * *

Perhaps I cannot write you because I want these associative links to stay mysterious. How will I explain where all of my potential communications have sprung from? I desire bond, not bondage. And perhaps, at times, the links are too perverse to elaborate with more interaction. In the corner of a loud and wooden bar, I have pulled my most glamorous and insightful friend's face close to my own. I want to ask her for ideas of what to write you, so why am I telling a story about my father who, several months ago, forwarded me my car registration in the mail? And then later that very night, I woke up to the sticker shredded on the floor, and I was shoving tiny Sephora Rewards sampler lotions and toners in my mouth? Sorry, what were we talking about?

* * *

A little mystery is good.

Un Buen Tiempo

Kleaver Cruz

Claribel tidied up the living room as much she could. La Lupe's raspy voice blasted through the speakers in the living room of the Reyes' two-bedroom apartment so loud the neighbors could hear her up and downstairs. A pain made its way from the back of Claribel's head down into her jaw. *Saturday morning music, but on a Friday night?* She knew better than to say anything about it. Her mother, Marysol, never cared about the neighbor's complaints or the headaches they gave Claribel.

Claribel took a deep breath. The twins were preoccupied: Jade spooned beef into discos with that bored and slouched posture of hers while Esme pressed in the edges of the soft dough with the precision of a surgeon. Claribel could already imagine them arguing that they'd done enough to get out of other chores that night. Of course, it landed on Claribel to make sure the rest of the apartment looked perfect.

Claribel reached her hand out to adjust a crooked frame slightly hidden behind the couch. The photo caught her eye—it was her mother, a young Marysol beaming a bright smile, arm in arm with another girl. The other girl's smile was beautiful too, her hair in a short-cropped afro. Claribel thought she recognized the girl. In the kitchen her mother's gold rings clinked, against iron pots of beans, white rice and pollo guisado. Marysol swayed her hips softly as she lip-synced along with the

Queen of Latin Soul. With the long silver serving spoon in her hand, she pushed the fluffy white rice in the large pot to the middle into a mound leaving the hardened rice underneath it to be exposed. Her eyes glazed over slightly, and a smile stretched across her face, "I can't wait to see Azula and her baby girl. It's been so long, too long."

"Here Ma, we're finished," Esme too swayed with La Lupe's voice, passing the ready-to-fry pastelitos.

"Thank you, my love," Marysol twirled her daughter before grabbing the container. "Clean up that table and wash whatever you used. Please."

Claribel sucked her teeth. She knew when her mother was active like she was tonight it was a bad idea to upset her visions of perfection. And as expected, the twins were squeamish at the thought of any more chores. Esme shrugged, swaying away with a smile, having left Jade at the kitchen table with a cup of foggy water, fork, greased spoon, the small squares of plastic from the discos packaging and the leftovers of ground beef in a small pot. Jade grunted a bit and stacked the items before putting them in the sink.

"Watch—you'll be stuck with the dishes next time. I promise," Jade spat the words at her twin's back under her breath, turned on the water and adjusted the knobs until it was cool enough to touch, but hot enough to kill the germs. Just like Marysol taught all her girls. Her small hands aggressively scrubbed the pot as she grit her teeth.

"Can you two just get along?" Claribel yelled over to the kitchen.

The twins nodded together from different rooms, "Sure!" Claribel sighed and walked past them with a knowing look. Marysol sang along loudly as she rinsed her hands over Jade's shoulders in the sink. Her voice echoed down the hall to the front door. The next Lupe song came on when the doorbell rang.

"They're here! Claribel, turn the music down! Better still, put on something else. Hurry up!" Marysol dried her hands and made her way to the door. With her head leaned against it, she asked,

"Who is it?"

"Azula y Yuri!" said a strangely familiar voice to Claribel from the other side of the threshold as her mother took a deep breath. If La Lupe had been spinning on a vinyl, her voice would have skipped just a half second in that moment. Marysol's confident posture masked the yearning for the warmth of her old friend. The woman at the door, Azula, had short black hair, and was about her age. Marysol stretched out her arms and hugged her perhaps too long. To Claribel, Azula's embrace was filled with love and a longing for somewhere beyond that moment. Behind Azula stood Yuri, smirking. She caught Yuri's eyes for a second and they both looked at their mothers.

"Come in, come in," Marysol ushered the two inside, then yelled down the hall, "Mi niñas, vengan aca! Come say hi!"

Claribel resisted the curve of the smile forming at the edges of her own lips, pretending to wait for an introductory cue.

"Clari, ven aca," Marysol pulled Claribel in front of their guests. Claribel resisted a little, then straightened herself out. Why did her mother always find the worst moment to treat her like a kid? "This is Azula and her baby Yuri. You probably don't remember them, but Azula was practically your Godmother when you were first born. We had big bellies at the same time. Went to doctor's appointments together. We did *everything* together growing up. Just running around and nobody could tell us anything. We were like sisters."

"We were thicker than thieves. Our souls were supposed to link up in this lifetime." The energy between the two women were like fridge magnets. Marysol stepped towards Yuri, gave her another squeeze and then stepped back in awe. "Que linda ta! Just beautiful," she said, taking in Yuri's 15-year-old self. "And this is my Claribel," she added, turning to Azula with pride.

"Hi, how you doing?" Claribel asked. Her voice came out high-pitched. She cleared her throat and forced herself to look from Yuri, beaming a smile at Azula instead. "Come here and give me a hug, Claribel. I held you in my arms when you were a baby." With Azula's arms tightened around her, Claribel caught a whiff of her mother's favorite Chanel No. 5 mixed with a powdery deodorant—unexpectedly comforting. "Dios mio, you're the spitting image of your mother." Azula's eyes pooled with awe. Claribel felt a mix of awkwardness, warmth, and a strange flutter in her chest.

Behind Marysol, Esme and Jade made noises with their closed fists, bumping each other they caught Claribel's glare and whispered, "K-I-S-S-I-N-G."

"Mi'ja, show Yuri around and get her something to drink. Chacha, no te ponga seca. Are you thirsty mama? We got soda, juice, water," she smiled a closed-mouth smile at Claribel and turned her head to Azula, "and for you we got some adult drinks," Marysol squeezed both her guests, "You're in your house now, don't be shy. Ok?" Crossing into the living-dining room, as the music blasted, Claribel could see Azula's eyes were somewhere else. The room swirled with deliciousness, the food, the smell of that signature perfume. Each scent and sound pulled her further back into memory.

Marysol said, "Claribel take care of whatever they need, me oye?"

Marysol nudged Claribel on the shoulder and pointed her nose down the hall. Claribel scanned Yuri's face for embarrassment, but she was calm, a slight grin tugging at the edges of her mouth.

"C'mon Yuri." Without thinking Claribel grabbed Yuri by the hand and led her further into the apartment. The twins followed close behind. Claribel looked down at her hand and, as if she did not recognize it, let go. "Can you two get off me?" Claribel said. "Go help Ma bring the food to the table."

"But we wanted to hang out with y'all," Esme said.

"With Yuri," Jade coughed into her hand.

"Go help Ma. *Now.*" She enjoyed telling off her sisters.

Yuri giggled softly as they entered. The small room oozed the scent of lavender and the remnants from the twins' experiments with nail polish. Claribel shook her hands to release this unfamiliar nervousness. Usually, people had to catch up to her.

"It looks different from what I imagined." As Yuri ran her finger along the edge of the round mirror on the center wall Claribel thought it might as well have been her spine. The glass' coolness contrasted the warm air coming through the open window.

"What did you imagine?" Claribel gave Yuri a curious look in the mirror.

Yuri turned to Claribel accidently stepping on her foot as Claribel steadied hers with Yuri's forearm feeling the hairs on her arm linger a second longer, she let go and stepped back tucking a loose braid behind her ear, trying not to smile. She looked at Yuri with a knowing smirk, "Try being 15 sharing a room with your 10-year-old twin sisters." Could Yuri hear her heart thumping in her stomach? Claribel tucked the notebook sticking out under her pillow and patted a spot on the bed for Yuri to sit and sat across from her, reaching for the black beret hanging from the bedpost.

"Do you watch *Doug*?" Claribel asked.

"The real question is who is your favorite character?"

"I don't think Judy gets enough love. Big sisters never do," Claribel said, posing with the beret in the mirror.

"Maybe it's because big sisters are annoying," Yuri smiled, "They always trying to love you and tell you what to do."

"Sometimes big sisters need big sisters." Claribel brushed an invisible piece of lint from her hat.

"I can't be your big sister, but I can be your friend," Yuri said. When she scooted closer their knees touched and a jolt shot through them, making both girls sit up straighter. Some silent rule broken.

"I'd like that," Claribel scooted back slightly, the wooden chair pressing against her skin—both a cool relief and a pang of mystery. Without realizing it, Claribel squeezed Yuri's palms, the mix of their callouses and soft spots comforted her.

"Claribel!" Marysol's voice rang from the kitchen. "Come help put this stuff on the table."

Claribel sucked her teeth and got up, "Let me get back into Big Sister mode."

While Claribel and Yuri moved dishes of steaming food to the table, Claribel watched her mother and old friend sitting closely, looking through the pictures Azula brought in a tattered envelope. The small rectangular images had taken on a sepia tone after decades of being trafficked behind sticky plastic in albums and different frames. Claribel's family only used that big dining table twice a year: Thanksgiving and Christmas. Otherwise, it was a token of status collecting dust, old mail, unused catalogues, and other small pieces of junk. This *was* a special occasion. It felt like a noche buena—a special gathering of family in every sense.

—

Read more of this novel excerpt online at asterixjournal.com

The Attic Is Missing

Aimee R. Cervenka

Guests were coming to dinner. This was such a routine occurrence that it scarcely required planning. Nevertheless, the family gathered in the kitchen to discuss what was to be done by whom. This too was routine.

Mother presided over the discussion, standing at the center island, her hands dancing through the air when she spoke. Even though most of the siblings had branched into some semblance of independence, they were obligated to return by a force so deeply embedded in their consciousnesses that none were fully aware of its existence. The older siblings suspected the sway their mother held over them, and they had begun to pull away as they matured. Still, the big house bound them as if to a web, which she herself was at the center of.

This newest engagement was yet another result of her tugging. Mother had begun to recognize the restlessness of her children, their desire to be free of her, but she knew something that they did not. She understood how their kind came into the world. She remembered how she and her mate had lovingly crafted their new home so many years ago. Like any male of good blood, he had sacrificed himself up to the structure when it was finished, allowing his flesh to become one with its walls. Only then had Mother been able to bring forth her children from the beams of the house infused with her lover.

Yet something had gone wrong. As the children moved away, they should have found mates and begun building their own houses, but they did not. They had moved into *apartments*, got jobs, had casual on-and-off relationships. She wondered if they lacked the instinct to build or had perhaps failed to attract appropriate partners. It was true, their kind had dwindled in numbers over the last few generations. What if there were no mates to be found? She pushed the thought away. They just needed focus. Were she to address the issue directly, however, it would do irreparable damage to their psyches. This was especially true of her sons, for it was important they come to such a decision of their own accord. Else, when the time came, they would fail to produce their own offspring. So instead, she found reasons to call them back again and again to the house, hoping it would influence them in some way. Still, she was getting older, and her children were becoming more resistant to her bidding. It had been months since she had last managed to gather them all to the house.

Tonight would be her last attempt to right her children.

* * *

The siblings rarely agreed on anything, so there was a great deal of shouting in the kitchen as each tried to be heard over the other. Maddie, as the oldest, believed that she inherently knew best. This irritated the others, who took it upon themselves to question each of her decisions. Derek, only a year younger, felt that he knew as much as she did and tried to best her where he could. When it had been his turn to move out of the house, he'd chosen to live twice as far away as Maddie had, though still within driving distance, of course. The twins, Robert and Richard, always sided only with each other. When one had decided to enroll at the local college, the other did too.

Mother thought it healthy for her children to have such arguments and, for the most part, stayed out of the discussion until final decisions were made. The social drudgery of a dinner party was only relevant to her insofar as it brought her children home and gave them something to do.

The current disagreement was about the salad dressing. Derek and Maddie were leaning toward a simple vinaigrette; the twins favored something creamier. The siblings knew that Mother wasn't going to weigh in, and none of the four seemed likely to concede.

Suddenly, Richard said, "Why don't we ask Anna?"

"Where is Anna?" asked Robert. The others looked around, surprised to realize that she wasn't amongst them.

* * *

Anna, as it happened, was upstairs. She was the youngest of the siblings and the only one who still lived in the house, being not quite old enough yet to make her own choices about such things. She had been tasked with putting away the boxes of Christmas decorations that had for weeks been sitting in a corner of the living room. Pulling down the ladder to do just this, she had looked up, expecting the dark, hot mouth of the attic, and seen nothing but empty sky.

Forgetting the boxes of decorations, Anna tumbled down the stairs and burst into the kitchen.

"The attic is gone," she said.

Ignoring her statement, Derek said, "Anna! We were just coming to find you."

Mother shepherded her into the kitchen. "You're needed as a tiebreaker, my dear. You really should try to be more involved." She worried most about Anna, who she'd barely managed to pull from the last of the house's reserves all those years ago.

"But the attic is missing!" Anna said again. She managed this time to catch the attention of the room.

"What do you mean 'missing'?" asked Mother.

Maddie waved her hand. "It's just another of her fancies."

Anna's siblings never took her seriously. "There's nothing there," she insisted. "Have a look for yourselves; it's easy enough to see."

As this seemed the simplest way to resolve the matter, the family moved toward the stairs, Anna trailing anxiously behind. Moments later, they were all standing at the base of the ladder, staring up in confusion.

"But where could it have gone?" asked Robert.

"My treasure!" cried Mother, which caused the siblings to share a look. They knew that nothing of value was kept in the attic. A few old boxes, decorations; mostly the space was filled with pink cotton-candy-like mounds of fiberglass insulation.

"We must call the police," she declared. She hurried back down the stairs, and the rest of the family followed.

An hour later, two officers knocked on the door. They were quickly ushered through the house to see the problem for themselves.

One of the officers, Officer Dally, turned to the family. "When was the last time you saw your attic?" If either was surprised by the situation, they hid it well.

Mother pulled at her lip. "I believe it was some time last week I was up there."

"And when did you notice it was missing?" asked Officer Dally.

Maddie pushed Anna forward, who looked down at the floor as she spoke. "I found it that way just this morning, sir. I was going to put those boxes there away, but when I pulled down the ladder..." Her voice trailed off.

They asked a few more questions and climbed to the top of the ladder to get a closer look. When they were finished, Dally looked to his partner, Officer Bis, who had remained silent to this point. Dally shrugged.

"Yes, all right," said Bis. "It is most definitely missing." He tapped his notebook. "We'll get this going down at the station and keep you posted."

They started to leave. On a whim, Mother stopped them. "We're having a dinner party this evening. Would you boys like to come?" She knew that a greater number of guests for the evening could only aid her endeavors. How her children hated a scene.

The officers started to refuse, but at that moment the smell of tomatoes and garlic slow-roasting in the oven wafted down the hall. Mother could be very persuasive. They verified the time of the gathering and promised that they would return. When they were gone, the family returned to the kitchen.

"Should we put up flyers in case someone finds it?" asked Anna.

"It's not like it's going to be floating around loose," Derek scoffed. "Someone's taken it."

"Who would do such a thing?" asked Richard.

Maddie tapped her fingers on the counter. "Don't forget that we need to finalize the place settings, and I'm still not sure about that butter sauce with the fish."

"The butter sauce will be fine," said the twins together.

The siblings continued to bicker in this way for some time. Of course, they were mostly concerned about how the guests would react to the missing attic and how they, in turn, would respond to those reactions. The police officers would be fine, even if none of the siblings understood why Mother had invited them; after all, they'd been so kind and helpful. But the Aronsons were coming from down the street. They wouldn't hesitate to share whatever they learned with the whole neighborhood. And the Daggs! What if they knew something about the attic or had been involved somehow? After all, it was the Daggs who'd stolen the family's dog last winter. They even dared to trot the poor thing around the block on occasion. His coat had been dyed a sort of reddish color, but it was definitely him.

The Peters were probably not to be trusted either. They were from another nice part of town, but no one could tell by looking at them. They loved to appropriate the drama of others. Given a week's time, the family would be hearing about their own unfortunate tale as if it had happened to the Peters instead.

"What if we just don't tell them?" suggested Richard.

Maddie rolled her eyes. "Don't you think they'll notice when they arrive?"

"It's not really visible from the road," Derek said. He'd already gone outside to check. "Besides, who knows when this happened. None of us noticed it when we got here."

Mother looked from one to the other of her children, her eyes bright.

Eventually it was decided that nothing would be said of the attic, and, if one of the guests were to bring it up, it would be discussed only in the most nonchalant of tones so as not to elicit glee or satisfaction in the less honorable of their guests.

Anna, who did not yet fully understand these kinds of things, asked, "Why do we invite them over if they create so many problems?"

Rather than answer such a question, her siblings looked around at each other and laughed. Mother smiled, secretly pleased by her smallest daughter's divergence. Perhaps she would yet awaken to her true nature.

Anna groaned and threw her hands up. "If anyone needs me, I'm going to put those boxes in one of the closets upstairs."

"Oh, that just won't do," someone said, but Anna had already left the room.

* * *

As the hour approached, the siblings settled into the rhythms of food preparation and table setting. Still, the first knock at the door startled them into a last-minute flurry.

Robert answered the door and found the police officers, returned as promised. He ushered them inside even as he wondered if inviting them on such short notice had been part of a greater scheme of Mother's. But what could her intentions possibly be? Certainly, she hadn't known the attic would go missing beforehand.

He followed the officers up the hallway but was stopped by a tug on his jacket. He turned to find Anna gesturing for him to follow. She led him into the darkened study and closed the door behind him.

She said, "Mother is up to something."

"Oh, not this." Robert reached to open the door, but Anna stopped him.

"You were thinking it, too. I could tell by the look you gave me." She stared at him, her eyes shining white in the dim lighting. As the youngest sibling, Anna had developed a sharper level of insight through observing the others, and she didn't hesitate to use it.

"Yes, all right. I was," he conceded. "I hate how you do that. But what on earth could her motive be?"

"What is always Mother's motive?"

"Attention. Right." Robert nodded. "But the attic? There's nowhere she could have put it. And she would have had to have had help. Do any of the others know anything?"

"Not that I can tell, though Maddie wouldn't share if she did." Anna rolled her eyes at the thought of her older sister.

Ignoring this, Robert added, "Richard would have told me if he'd heard anything. But what can we do except wait to see how it plays out?"

"I know. I just hate how she does this. I don't know why all of you even come back."

Robert smiled wistfully at his little sister. He was by now old enough to recognize Mother's pull as something beyond his control. "We come back because we must. You will too, you'll see."

"I won't," she said stubbornly, but she followed him out of the study.

* * *

The grand Victorian-style house gleamed in the evening light as the rest of the guests made their way up the drive. It had been built on a slight incline, placing it above and apart from the other houses on the street, so that anyone climbing up to the house felt as if they were simultaneously departing from the neighborhood below them. Rose bushes lined the front walkway, but not a single tree adorned the yard; they had all gone into the building of the house.

In the dining room, the siblings carried platters of food to the table as the last of the guests were seated.

"Everything looks wonderful," said Liza Peter. There was murmured agreement.

The siblings had, as usual, outdone themselves. There was a mixed greens salad with bits of pear and walnut in a lemon vinaigrette, crostini drizzled with olive oil and roasted tomatoes, wedges of sharp cheese arranged with slices of smoked summer sausage, and bite-sized tartlets filled with bits of roast vegetables and parmesan cheese.

"Please help yourselves," said Mother. "These are just the starters, of course, so make sure you save room."

Dinner continued in this manner. The conversation was artificially pleasant, the food and drink of good quality. The siblings spoke only to their guests, but shared glances with one another across the table. For the main course, they had prepared thin fillets of white fish in a garlic butter sauce, pork medallions braised in wine, a mound of crisp-skinned fingerling potatoes, and asparagus spears shining with olive oil and flaky salt. Thick slices of crusty bread for sopping juices were passed in a bowl around the table.

Officer Dally groaned appreciatively as he took another bite of pork. "I say, Bis, we lucked out today."

"Mmhm," Bis agreed, his mouth full of potatoes.

Michael Aronson turned to them. "And how do you know our wonderful hosts?"

Anna looked to Robert as they both clicked to understanding. The officers' presence guaranteed that the attic would come up. It was only natural that their guests would attempt to ferret out why such strangers had been invited amongst them.

"Let's bring out dessert," said Derek. The siblings jumped from their chairs and hurried to the kitchen. Pastries and sliced fruit were piled on trays at the ready.

"This is a disaster," Maddie hissed as soon as they were out of earshot.

Anna glanced at Robert. "We think Mother did it."

Derek scowled. "Don't be ridiculous."

"That's why she invited the police," Robert said. "Think about it." Richard nodded slowly in agreement with his twin.

Leaning over the counter, Maddie put her head in her hands and shut her eyes. She groaned.

"Maddie?" asked Anna.

Maddie didn't respond. When she straightened, her hands were balled into fists at her sides. She grabbed a platter and marched back into the dining room. The others followed.

"How terrible," Sanda Dagg was saying. "I just assumed you were having work done."

Maddie dropped her tray of melon none too gently on a corner of the table. Guests and family alike turned to stare at her. "Mother." Her voice was sharp and controlled. "What have you done with the attic?"

Alarmed, Derek moved to stop his sister. Whispers fluttered between the guests.

Mother's mouth quirked, and a bubble of laughter escaped from her lips. So, they'd found her out. Perhaps that meant they were beginning to understand. This thought only made her more certain of what she had set in motion. She drew something from beneath the napkin on her lap and clutched it to her breast. A look none of the siblings had ever seen before took hold of her features as she pushed herself back from the table.

She stood and shook her fist at the gathering, the object in her hand flashing as she did so. It was the latch that had held the attic door.

Richard started to ask, "Is that...," but seeing her children's eyes upon the small object, Mother lifted it to her mouth, pushed it past her lips, and swallowed. She beamed at her guests-turned-audience.

"That's better," she said. "It's such a shame to leave things unfinished."

The officers glanced at each other. Dally asked, "Ma'am, did you...eat your attic?"

"Isn't that what you're supposed to figure out?" she quipped. She felt herself swelling with the urgency of what she needed to do. She was pleased with the progress she'd already made and was not about to diminish the process. Not with so much at stake.

At that moment, the siblings wanted nothing more than for the guests to leave so that they could turn their energies to addressing this new situation. The guests, however, wanted nothing more than to stay. They watched with silent attention, as if this were a sort of planned entertainment for the evening. Maddie motioned for her brothers and sister to follow her into the kitchen while the officers continued their attempt to interrogate Mother.

"Now what?" Richard asked when no one else spoke.

"I can't believe her!" Maddie exclaimed.

Anna asked, "Do you want me to go see if she ate the ladder too?" The others merely looked at her. "I mean, the latch was there earlier," she continued, "and now it's clearly not. She all but said it was the last piece, so…"

"Ugh!" said Maddie. She waved her hands at her sister. "Yes, fine. Go check." Anna left.

While this exchange was taking place, Derek had begun to feel the hint of an idea rising from some buried place in his mind. "What if she's planning to consume the house?"

"But why?" asked Robert. *How* was hardly important. The siblings knew that if Mother wanted to do a thing, she would.

An understanding was slowly forming in Maddie's mind as well. "She's been restless for a long time," she said. "I think it's Father."

For the siblings, the suggestion was a grave one. The topic of their father was strictly forbidden. Mother had never told them anything about him, and they had known from an early age not to ask. Each of the children in their own time had come to question whether he had even existed.

Richard was the first to speak. "How can you be sure?"

Maddie started to answer when they heard Anna on the steps. Robert put a finger to his lips. "Don't tell her about this," he said. "It will only scare her."

"But what do we *do* about it?" Derek asked.

Before anyone could respond, Anna reentered the kitchen. "Yep, it's gone."

"We have to get all of these people out of here," said Robert. A sense of urgency rippled through the kitchen.

"This will ruin us," Maddie muttered to herself. Then, as loudly as she could, she shouted, "Everyone, quick! The roof over the garage has disappeared too!"

As she had hoped, the guests crowded into the entryway. Once everyone was outside, she locked the front door. "Someone lock the back," she directed. One of the siblings sprang to her bidding.

The guests soon realized the diversion for what it was. When they couldn't get back in, they gathered around the dining room windows, pressing their hands against the glass to peer in. Officer Bis rapped on the glass. "We need to ask a few more questions," he shouted.

Mother stood staring around the room in anticipation. She pretended not to notice her audience as she listened to her children calling out to one another in panic. Good, she thought. That meant they knew she was serious.

She waited until they had hurried back into the room, their eyes upon her. Then, she reached out and pulled one of the slats from the wooden blinds. She put the end of it into her mouth and began to chew. The familiarity that washed through her was almost overwhelming. When she had begun to consume the attic, she had been shocked by the taste of her lover. Each mouthful brought him back to her. She continued to eat. Within moments, the length of the slat was gone. She reached for another.

Anna cried out, "Mother! What are you doing? This is our home!"

Something of Anna's cries pulled at her distanced older sister. Maddie stepped forward and took her arm. "Anna, there's nothing we can do."

"But why is she—" Anna stopped speaking. Her mother pulled off chunks of the drywall, working steadily through them. Anna looked around at her siblings and felt the loss in their expressions radiate through her.

Robert spoke gently, his voice full of knowing, "She's ending things." Anna looked around. The others nodded in hushed agreement, but for her, this idea was incomprehensible. Her mother was still strong and forceful. More importantly, she loved them.

Anna crossed the room, stepping over the splinters of debris that littered the floor. She grabbed hold of Mother's arm. "Please, stop this," she all but whispered.

Mother had been watching her children speak, but unable to hear their conversation over the sound of her own chewing, she dared to hope they had reached something of the realization she wanted for them. What else could bring them together in such quiet understanding and unity of purpose? When Anna came to her, she felt that she would burst with joy. Her children and her line would continue. She placed the length of baseboard she had been eating against a chair and pulled her daughter into her arms.

She spoke into her daughter's dark hair, "My dear, I have no choice but to finish. I do so happily, knowing I have succeeded and my beautiful children will flourish. Do not worry for me; I go to be with your father now."

To Anna, Mother's words were like the ramblings of a stranger. She stumbled free of her grip and fled to her siblings. They encircled her, pulling her from the room.

Mother crooned after them, a long, low, wordless sound. She spun around the room, once, before abandoning herself wholly to her task, pulling the exposed beams from the walls and lifting them to her mouth.

Derek winced at the sight. "Come now, it won't be safe soon. There's nothing more to be done here."

"What do we do about them?" Richard gestured toward the windows.

Maddie waved her hand, exhausted. "They'll get bored or scared and leave. I can't care anymore." The outer wall of the dining room had begun to sag, causing the floor above to shudder and sway.

They left reluctantly, making their way across the damp front lawn.

Anna gazed at the collapsing house, Mother somewhere inside. "But what do I do now?" she asked.

Robert stopped and put an arm around her shoulders. A thought tickled at the back of his mind like the tugging of a single silvered thread. "I suppose now you'll build your own house. We all will."

"Can I stay with you until then?"

"Of course," he said.

As Anna looked back a last time, something inside her broke loose and bubbled up through the uncertainty and loss that had filled her a moment before. A quiet smile crept across her face. Anna would build her house or she wouldn't. The choice was entirely her own. She turned away from the place of her birth and followed her siblings down the lamp-lit street.

Who We Walk With

Alba Delia Hernández

Dime con quién andas y te diré quién eres

1

Conciencia was born with the map of Puerto Rico on her thigh. The main island and the neighboring small islands of Vieques, Culebra, Desecheo, Mona, Caja de Muertos and over a hundred even smaller islands, islets and cays took the shape of white vitiligo spots on Conciencia's dark brown skin. Her skin glistened as if she had bathed in a tub of liquid gold. When she gets older, her high cheekbones will give off a bloody red glow. One of her almond shaped eyes had white eyelashes that when she blinked it looked like tiny butterflies were sprinting on her face.

2

Doña Nina got into the foster care system because she cared about children. When Conciencia was presented to her, she knew that she would love this seven-year-old child who looked like she could be her own child.

Things were different in this home. Conciencia did not slam doors or kick chairs. The first day she was sent to live with Doña Nina, she made Conciencia guava empanadas. She looked at the empanadas then at Doña Nina.

"Come, niña. I made them for you."

Conciencia was hungry and bit into the warm and gooey guava. Mmmmmmm. She had never tasted something so good. Her tummy was filled. Doña Nina gave her another and another until Conciencia fell asleep with her head folded on the table.

Doña Nina may have been overweight, diabetic and had a compromised heart, but she was strong enough to carry Conciencia's eighty-pound body to the twin bed she had bought just for her. She wiped the guava gel from Conciencia's cheeks and blessed her before going into her room and praying to the many saints she worshiped.

Conciencia's hair had been cut to the scalp, like a boy's buzz cut. The six children in the foster home had gotten lice and cutting their hair was an expected course of action. But even before the lice, Conciencia's hair had been cut short. Conciencia didn't like combing her hair and fought when anyone else tried doing so. No one knew how to unknot her hair. But things were different in this new home. Doña Nina boiled onions and used the onion water with coconut oil to massage Conciencia's scalp. After two months Conciencia's thick strong black hair began to grow. Doña Nina taught Conciencia to untangle her hair with her fingers while she was in the bath. Every week she deep conditioned it with mayonnaise and eggs. No longer did Conciencia have to feel the knuckles of someone frustrated with Conciencia's *ouch* and *aii*. When Conciencia's hair was long enough, Doña Nina taught her how to braid her own hair. Conciencia loved this look the most. For the first time ever, at the age of eleven, she looked in the mirror and saw someone pretty. By the time she was twelve, she wore her hair in two thick braids that made her stand out from everyone in the crowd.

Doña Nina taught her how to cook, how to make the masa for the empanadas. Soon they were making a business out of their home, selling empanadas de queso, de pollo, y de guava y queso. They sold them three for one dollar. Conciencia would do everything to create the masa, made of flour, butter, water and her secret ingredient, brown sugar. She shaped them like a pregnant belly and gave them their forked ridges. Doña Nina would fry them because she did not think Conciencia understood the danger of fire.

Conciencia finally had someone she could call Mamá. Someone with large bosoms to lean against. Someone to bring slippers to. Someone who didn't have a large voice, instead she said Conciencia's name the way it was meant to be said, like gentle waves coming from her mouth with a sweetness like her guava empanadas.

One night Doña Nina woke up screaming, "No! No!" and ran to Conciencia's room and they both knelt down while Doña Nina prayed in a way that Conciencia couldn't understand. She wasn't even really praying. She was begging. When Conciencia asked her what was wrong, she shook her head, "Pray with me, pray."
Doña Nina didn't want her to know that she had dreamt that she carried Conciencia's infant body to the third-floor window and accidentally

dropped her three flights down. She woke up begging, "God no!"

Two days later when Conciencia had just finished eating her oatmeal before going to school, Doña Nina smiled fully and told her, "You're going to be okay. Last night I dreamt that you were riding the white horse of Santa Barbara. You'll be okay. There will be forces that will try to destroy you because you are going to be very powerful, but do not worry, Yemaya and Santa Barbara will protect you. Pray to them. Que bueno que Santa Barbara te escogió a ti como soldada fiel. Santa Barbara has chosen you to be one of her trust.

3

Conciencia was put into special education classes just a few months into first grade. She was placed in a room with children that threw chairs against walls and favored the word 'fuck' over all other words. Sweet Conciencia, a quiet little girl with her head down and with a side glance was placed with the *poster-children for prophylactics*, as one teacher put it. Conciencia was kept in this class since the first grade because despite all attempts, she wouldn't learn English.

"What day of the week are we in?" Her head down.

"Is it raining outside or sunny?" Shrugged shoulders.

"Your name? Conciencia? What mother would name a child that?" The teacher muttered.

It wasn't all failure or waste of time. By fifth grade Conciencia had learned how to stick her middle finger out, shout, and chase her classmates. Poor Mrs. Neally, the new teacher who came so prepared with her lesson plans and wide blue eyes, tried to teach them what verbs and nouns were. She was the only teacher who truly cared for them. The poor woman spent half of her lunch break crying in the ladies' bathroom.

Conciencia learned to turn tables upside down, to hide in the wooden closet. She practiced robot dance moves. "Do the pump," her classmates demanded, and she danced, her chest pounding to the beat of her friends' fists against desks. Little by little, she learned to speak English and stand with her chest as high as her chin, "Yeah motherfucker," she told Corey who towered over her, "you have a problem with me, yeah, well fix this problem! You black slave." And everyone laughed, *ha ha!* And Corey would respond, "Yeah, spic, take a fucking bath and get some socks. It's winter. And you blacker than me stupid."

"Yeah," Conciencia said, laughing so much she was barely understandable, "I saw a pig fucking your momma."

"I saw your momma sucking a pig's dick," Corey answered back.

They went on and on. There was no fighting. They all stood together in this class. But God forbid someone from another class messed with them. That rarely happened. They had named their class, their crew— The Innocents, because as Corey said, "We are innocent until proven guilty."
Sandra, who was two years younger than the rest of them, but taller than all of them, was either under her desk or standing on it.

Julio cried for a reason no one could understand. He would hide in the closet to cry and when he came out, he was angry, kicked chairs and fought anyone who would come near him. He sat in a corner of the room, and everyone knew to leave him alone until he was ready to join them.

Angel was put in special education classes because even at the age of eleven, he read as if he had rocks in his mouth, vowels trying to roll over the rocks and consonants drilling holes into them. His long hair covered his sad honey-colored eyes. Because of the way he whisked his hair away from his face, a few boys in the hallway whispered, "Is he a faggot?"

There was Melinda who came to school with spray paints and tagged the tables whenever the teacher turned her back. Mrs. Neally would ignore the sound and smell of the spray and kept writing on the board. Nobody told on Melinda. In her long bathroom breaks, with Conciencia as guard, she painted a mural that included flowers, an ocean and the words 'fuck you' in turquoise.

Their classes were relegated to the third floor, the side of the building where the sun shone most. There were swinging doors separating them from the regular education classrooms. Regular Ed students looked through the small square windows on the metal doors to get a peek at students who were just hanging around or sitting on the hallway radiator. Sometimes the smell of cigarettes would sift through the doors. The best days were when they could get a look at a fight or a wooden desk being thrown against the wall.

4

The first time Juanito entered Conciencia's classroom, they all looked at him as if he were the fish they were trying to bait. A new kid to taunt and beat to see how much heart he really had. He grew his dark hair into a short, tightly curled afro. On his chest gleamed a gold medallion with the island of Puerto Rico on it. When the teacher left the classroom to investigate the commotion in the hallway, Conciencia and Corey, leading the group, surrounded Juanito.

"Hey punk," Corey said, "you speak English?"

Juanito reached into his right sock and with one quick movement, brandished a shiny blade. Corey looked at Conciencia.

Conciencia told Juanito, "Put that blade away before the teacher comes back in."

After the three o'clock bell and they were outside, Conciencia told Juanito, "Join us. We're The Innocents."

Juanito had more muscles than anyone else. His chest could not help but stretch the buttonholes of his green shirt.

"Why are your eyelashes white?"

Conciencia didn't answer him. Instead, she asked again, "Well, do you want to be part of us?"

"Who's the leader?" he asked.

"I'm the leader. This is the last time I will ask."
They shook on it. They walked home together and realized that they live on the same block.

"There are six rules to follow. You have to memorize them."

1) No fighting between us.

2) If anyone messes with any of us, we'll be there to defend our friend and be part of the retaliation, if necessary.

3) All members' book bags and notebooks will have The Innocents graffitied on it by Melinda.

4) I am the head of the group. If you have problems with someone else in the group, tell me about it.

5) If any of us come to school hungry, then the ones who can will sneak in food for them. You can count on me for guava empanadas.

6) If anyone needs clothes, Sandra's mom knows how to sew.

"Why are you in charge?" Juanito asked.

Conciencia replied, "Because I can read and write in English and because I can fight."

5

There was no explanation given as to why the broken window in Conciencia's class was never fixed or boarded up. The whole rectangular window including the wooden pane was missing. Kids sometimes threw books out there. Sometimes they spit just to watch their saliva go down four flights. Through the frame of the window they could see the block across the street: There were only three buildings there. Two of the buildings were abandoned. One of them looked like it had been sliced horizontally in half. You could only see the first floor and only one window on the second floor of a six-family home apartment building. Next to it was a building missing a roof. Sometimes teenagers playing hooky snuck inside them. The third one did have people living in there. One could tell because a Puerto Rican flag hung from the third-floor window. Surrounding the buildings there was gray rubble, junk yards and dust rising from the rubbish.

6

Conciencia became the best reader of the class. Maybe it was because she had finally found a stable foster home, and more than anything she wanted Doña Nina to be proud of her.

On a day that Conciencia was looking out the window the assistant principal, Mrs. Smith, asked her to follow her to her office.

Conciencia sat in the office and stared at a framed photo of Mrs. Smith's family. Her children, three of them with blue eyes like their mom's sitting around a huge Christmas tree, bigger than any that Conciencia had ever seen. Her husband smiled, pointing at the Rudolph nose on his sweater. Conciencia sat on a wooden chair that rocked every time she moved. Mrs. Smith sat behind her desk with papers organized and clean. An office with no window.

"I have good news for you," Mrs. Smith said with a smile. "You scored on a ninth-grade reading level on your state tests."

Conciencia, who wasn't fond of showing emotion to adults, said nothing.

"First though, I have to ask this question. Did anyone help you with the exam?"

Conciencia was taken aback. There was a teacher there the whole time. The seats were spread out so no one would cheat. "No," she finally answered.
"Ok then, we have decided that we will place you in Mr. Singer's class, where you belong now."

"You mean, you're switching my class?"

"That class will be more appropriate for you. You're going to love it there."

Conciencia thought of throwing Mrs. Smith's family picture against the wall but decided against it.

Mrs. Smith walked Conciencia back to her classroom and asked her to grab her things.

Everyone including Juanito and Corey asked, "What's going on?" "Come now, Conciencia," Mrs. Smith insisted.

"I'm not leaving," she said, drumming her fingers on her desk.

"My child, you don't have a choice."

Mrs. Smith used the phone inside a metal box against the wall to call security.

Mr. Banner, the 6' 4" gym teacher that most students were afraid of arrived first. "All right, let's go sweet tart," he told Conciencia.

She didn't respond.

"Do you need some help getting up?" he asked.
Conciencia turned her head and looked out the open window. Mr. Banner put a hand on her shoulder. "Get up on your own or I'll carry you myself," he shouted, "This is my lunch period."

Mrs. Neally tried to intervene, "Maybe give her a day to think about it?"

"Take your hand off my shoulder," Conciencia said through clenched teeth. She looked back at Juanito, who was rubbing his hands together as if he were trying to make fire.

"All right," Mr. Banner said with a smile. "I guess you'll have to be dessert." He yanked Conciencia's elbow and tried to lift her, but Conciencia had wrapped her legs around the legs of her desk. Her body, chair and desk fell to the floor, her head taking the brunt of the fall. "Get your hands off her," Juanito shouted.

The security guard arrived and held Conciencia's arms, Mr. Banner held her legs.

Juanito asked Corey to repeat rule number two. "If anyone messes with any of us, we'll be there to defend our friend and be part of the retaliation, if necessary."

At this, Juanito, Corey, Julio, Sandra, Melinda and Jonathan got up. They grabbed their chairs and began to strike Mr. Banner. He was hit so hard that he dropped his hold of Conciencia. Corey took off his belt and struck the security guard in the face with the metal buckle. Mrs. Neally was in the hallway crying for help. The assistant principal was nowhere to be seen. The whole class, except for Angel, got up and pummeled the security guard and gym teacher.

In less than ten minutes, the police arrived and the whole class, even Angel, who had done nothing, were handcuffed, faces against the board, chalk dust painting their skins white.

7

Conciencia prepared the empanadas that Doña Nina taught her to make. She looked forward to surprising her and Doña Nina's two friends as they returned from Sunday Mass. Conciencia had filled the empanadas with beef and potatoes and on a separate plate her favorite empanadas, the sweet guava and white cheese ones. She used a dish towel to wipe the sweat off her forehead. It was a 100-degree July day. The only thing to cool them off was a window fan that she turned off because it was making the paper napkins flutter across the counter. She focused on creating perfect ridges around the half-moon shape of the empanadas, so focused that she forgot about the oil bubbling in the pan. When she turned around a fire was blazing taller than she was. She knelt, picked up one of her chancletas and tried to put the fire out. Instead, the fire attacked her blouse. Her skin. She dropped to the floor unconscious. The fire spread to the walls.

Juanito was playing handball on the courts on Troutman Street when he saw the smoke rising.

"Conciencia's house is on fire!" his friend Pito yelled.

Juanito ran fast toward it, his legs felt like rubber.

People covered their noses. "Where are the fire trucks? ¿Donde están los bomberos?" People cried.

Juanito tried to enter from the front wooden doors, lit like logs in a fire pit. Juanito took off to the apartment building to the left where the front doors were never locked and had a basement door that flung freely. He ran down the basement stairs, ran up the stairs that led to the yard, climbed over the yard fence to Conciencia's yard, jumped on the window ledge and elbowed the window fan till it fell. He could see Conciencia on the kitchen floor. The fire had risen, but saints conspired in whispers and left the ground where Conciencia lay untouched.

He crawled on the ground, grabbed Conciencia by her arms and dragged her over the window ledge. He carried her body down the basement stairs and out of the building. Once outside he yelled, "Help, help, help me!"

There was smoke. Coughs. Men, children and women crying. Another building caught fire.

People sliced the air with their hands as if cutting cane, shouting, "Where the fuck are the fire trucks? ¿Dónde está la ambulancia?"

Juanito knelt over Conciencia's body, "Wake up Conciencia. Wake up."

The flesh of her chest was exposed like a pink carnation. There was a smell like burnt pork, burnt hair and another foul smell Juanito had never experienced before. One of the neighbors, Indio, got his car and helped Juanito carry Conciencia's body into his car. "We're taking her to the hospital ourselves," Indio yelled.

Juanito sat in the backseat with Conciencia on his lap. "Wake up, Conciencia." His chest heaved like a wrath filled wave. He checked her wrist for a pulse the way he had seen on TV. He was sure he could feel one. He held Conciencia gently in his arms. He bathed his head in the smoke rising from her body and chanted, "Let the smoke cleanse my mind. The most important thing right now is that Conciencia lives. If she lives, I will stop smoking, stop stealing, stop fighting, stop skipping school, dear God, dear Lord Jehovah or Jesus, God. Ven, ven, Papa Dios, aquí. Ven, Papa Dios. Curala, Señor, curala." He sobbed in the mist of her body.

At the hospital, she was left on a stretcher in the hallway. Above her, a gap in the ceiling, powdered dust on her body. Cockroaches zig-zagged across the floor. When Juanito screamed at everyone in the emergency room, an attendant screamed back, "We are doing the best we can!"

If it hadn't been for Juanito, Conciencia would've perished. The firemen had been busy putting out a fire in the neighboring community of Ridgewood, where historic brownstones stood and Puerto Ricans weren't welcome. By the time the fire trucks finally made it to Bushwick, four buildings and the old lady on the third floor of Conciencia's building, who never left her apartment, had been consumed by the fire.

Conciencia for the rest of her life did not grow breasts. Instead on her chest blossomed a black orchid, a shield that protected Conciencia's heart from any further suffering.

—

Read more of this novel excerpt online at asterixjournal.com

Real Americans

Dionne Ford

The walkway to Dona Rosa's front door is overgrown with roses. At first, I think I've come to the wrong place. But the tile inserted into the high stucco wall overrun with bougainvillea and geraniums, says 12 Rua do Jardim in bright blue enamel. That's the address José gave me. I look up and down the street before I open the wrought iron gate, painted white and rusting at the joints and along the handle. No one is coming.

"Look at me! Look at me," the flowers seem to scream, "just don't hurt me." I lift their blooming, heavy heads out of my way. Maybe Dona Rosa will let me cut some roses for her, even let me take a few home with me. A pink one for Dorys's dinner table. A white one for Violeta's altar. A red one for Claudio's, well, everything.

The home is smaller than I expected, and not new like the others on this street, reminding me of my granny's one stubborn baby tooth in the front of her mouth that refuses to budge. Andrea lives over in this new development—her family is hosting Chris, the other American exchange student with the surf punk hairdo—and Claudio's cousin lives over in this part of Little America too. They have live-in maids but the Bissacos just have Dona Lucia who comes a few times a week and goes home at the end of the day.

I guess I was imagining something more like the old Ford Mansion back home in Akinville where George Washington stayed the winter before we beat the British. Or the big house on the sugar plantation just at the edge of this city's limits where I was invited to a party the first week I got here, four months ago already. Drinking Guaraná on the patio, I was reminded of why Washington picked Akinville for his winter camp. From its mountain views, he could see the British coming on the river below. The big house, too, sits above Little America looking down on everybody—subject or enemy.

A huge confederate flag hangs inside the front window. I roll my eyes. It's not supposed to affect me, because, people say, it doesn't mean the same thing here as it does back home. The screen door is closed, so I call out instead of using the doorbell the way Ana Cásia does when we go to visit her grandparents or the way Andrea does when she comes to invite me to her house for a swim.

"Boa tarde, Dona Rosa," I say into the blackness beyond the metal bars and the mesh screen. A sudden breeze sweeps across the porch into the tree pressing against it, sliding out a whistle from between its leaves. I shiver. The tree feels familiar. Being from the Garden State, I feel like I should know what it's called, but I can't think of its name. I do however know the smell wafting out from the house. Cornbread. My great-granny's was the best. She made it with buttermilk, let it cool on her speckled countertop, and before I could even ask, she'd slide me thin slices of it that I ate right from the knife's blade.

A high creaking voice calls from the back of the house. "Boa tarde. Quem é?" Has she forgotten that I'm supposed to come? Or did she just forget my name?

"It's Deenie, the exchange student," I say. "The one staying with José and Dorys, the Bissacos?"

A silver-headed woman emerges from the back of the house, leaning hard on a cane, a multi-colored crocheted shawl sagging from her thin shoulders. She unlocks the screen with a key and grabs my hand with a tight squeeze, then gives it a swing instead of a shake. "Boa tarde, minha filha. Boa tarde. I wasn't expecting someone who could speak Portuguese." She touches my cheek with her damp crumpled hand and calls me "Sugar," sounding just like my New Orleans family, and I feel proud, then bashful, and immediately want to please her.

I straighten the collar of my sleeveless shirt and speak in my best Portuguese pronunciation before she can show me to her little sitting room where teacups, cookies and cornbread wait on flowered China plates and saucers.

"Que ótimo, Dona Rosa to learn about the history of Little America from a real American Brazilian. Excelente!" This tickles Dona Rosa until her spotted face turns bright pink and she works herself up to a coughing spell, then collapses into a high back chair to recover. I offer to get her some water from the kitchen, but she says no. She wants to feel the heat of laughter on her face and in her lungs.

"Senta-se. Senta," she commands, batting at the air until I sit down in a chair that matches hers. She pours us cups of tea, gives us each a cube of brown sugar, then pops a square of the cornbread into her mouth. I do the same which makes us both happy. The house itself may be played out, but everything in it seems priceless for all the care that someone, Dona Rosa or the maid, has taken with it. The China gleams and the picture frames shine silver with none of those black streaks that always stain my family's few pieces until we have company. And the cornbread is perfect—browned on top and golden inside.

There is silence while she pours and I realize this would have been the proper time to present her with a lovely bouquet of roses, like the ones taking over her yard. I take the stick pin from my pocket with the Akinville town seal on it and set it on her mahogany coffee table. "Dona Rosa, that's just a little something from my town, Akinville, New Jersey," I say. I give the raised bump on my shin a quick rub. Either the ointment or my jeans rubbing against the Band-Aid make it itch.

"Deixa ver," she says and holds out her hand. I place it there gently, to make it seem like it's more valuable, more precious than it really is and she brings it up close to her face, gives it a long hard look and then holds it up to the single stream of sunlight filtering into the room. She coos over it while she twirls it in the sun ray, tells me she's so happy to have it and that Akinville must be a beautiful place. "I want it on my shawl," she says, "so I can show it off." I stick it there between some of the more tightly knitted pieces of yarn and wonder whom she has to show it off to.

"How do you like our town?" she says, and I say fine, but my eyes wander over to the confederate flag covering the window, then the picture on the wall next to it.

"Real Americans like you and me," Dona Rosa says, pointing to the picture. "Bring it here." I retrieve the picture from the wall and see Dona Rosa and a bunch of people dressed in hoop skirts and confederate uniforms smiling for the camera, crumbling tombstones jutting out of the grass behind them.

"This was at the Festa Confederada last year." She rubs her crooked index finger over the picture and leaves a smudge across the faces of the Americans. "Que saudades," she says and I wonder who in the picture has left her, who it is that she's now missing.

Common Sense Rule #19. Nostalgia for home is to be expected. Write letters to family and friends often to keep the blues at bay.

I miss my magenta bangs—mom made me cut them before I left. I miss rehearsing for the spring musical—I would have had a real chance for a lead, not just the chorus, now that I'm in eleventh grade. I miss the cornbread and ham my family will have next week for Thanksgiving. But mostly I miss Emma, the way I could tell her anything. That night last year after rehearsal for *Anything Goes,* I called her, crying and hyperventilating into the phone. I was one of Reno Sweeney's Angels and I had made the mistake of telling my mom I was nervous that we were going to each have a little part to sing solo. That got my mom going on her high school days, how popular she was even though she was the only Black girl in the whole place, how she was all set to be a famous singer. Over spaghetti and meat sauce for me, three glasses of Gallo wine for her, Mom told me that she never really wanted children, and that my father had talked her into "domesticity." Then, she held my hands like we were girlfriends and said, "Don't let anyone steal your dreams, Deenie." That's when I decided to get the hell out of that house, that town, that country—all places that demanded my gratitude and appreciation even though I never asked to be there. I never asked to be at all. Emma didn't judge me when I said I couldn't wait to be rid of them all. The night of the knife, Emma still didn't judge. I was just trying to defend my mom since it was partly my fault that she'd been forced into something she didn't want and I felt sorry for her. Still, Mom found a way to blame me. Not Emma. She just said her family goes crazy sometimes too and it was probably good to get some space and some time away. Now it's been a season since I last saw my parents. I guess I kind of miss them too even though I came here to get away from them, the mess of their marriage, their total disinterest in me and all of our... misunderstandings. But here in Brazil—the only one of the twenty-three International Exchange Club countries that would have me—I wonder. Have I really escaped anything?

Dona Rosa lightly pats my knee. "You'll come this year. It's a wonderful celebration. The whole town participates and we Confederados dress up in our American clothes and eat our American food."

I blow at my tea and picture her and the other Confederados out in an open field surrounded by hamburgers and hot dogs, apple pie and milk. It was my second day in the country when Ana Cásia told me about them and so they were the first thing I wrote down on my list of New Portuguese Words. Confederados: The US southerners who came to southern Brazil after the Civil war and founded Little America, São Paulo.

"What kind of American food do you make, Dona Rosa? Do you bring this delicious cornbread?"

"Obrigada, filha. Yes. That's my grandmother's recipe. We have cornbread, watermelon, fried chicken, vinegar pies," she says and I smile to myself at how what she calls American food is really Southern food, soul food, and I like that she is as proud of her "Confederate" heritage as I am of my New Orleans roots.

"It's some party. All the newspapers come and sometimes the TV stations. And of course the mayor," and she raises her palms at his name, like he's an obligation she has to suffer, the way I imagine she did when the International Club phoned to say another American exchange student would darken her door. "We even had an American president once. But he wasn't president then. He was just a governor from Georgia. Somebody he was related to was buried at the Campo Cemetery."

With the cornbread all gone, I take a sip of tea to wash down the stale biscoito, victim of the relentless heat here or the air conditioning—I haven't discovered yet which is the culprit spoiling baked goods overnight. "Jimmy Carter?"

Dona Rosa looks up quickly. "How did you know?"

I shrug my shoulders and don't mention how obsessed I was with Amy Carter having that entire white house to play in, or how my parents were always talking about how finally there was a real God-fearing man running the land.

"Que bom," she says, tapping her finger on the side of her head before pointing at me. "Smart girl."

I don't know about smart. It's more that I pay attention. How else to stay safe? I wonder, but don't ask if Dona Rosa has ever voted.

"Was it hard to live under military government, Dona Rosa?" She laughs hard again, but stops short of coughing.

"They're in control, filha just like any other government, just like your so-called democracia." She nods her head at me now, like she's caught me in a lie. "Oh yes, that nice man from Georgia was the only

American president to tell our government he didn't like the way we were doing business, torturing the subversivos who spoke against the military, running the military presidents out of the country when they were no longer useful. All the other presidents before him, they liked our military government just fine. To me, they're all the same. Maybe with Tancredo, God rest his soul, things could have changed, but with this guy now, Sarney, he used to be with the military too. How's he any different?"

I get quiet the way everyone does here whenever the dead president Tancredo Neves is mentioned. He was to be the first democratic president after 20 years of military government, or as Dorys likes to say, he was a little bit of gold after all those anos de chumbo, but he dropped dead the night before his job was supposed to begin. His funeral lasted for days.

Dona Rosa waves a fly away from her head and lets out a sigh. "Democracia, ditadura, what does it matter? I go on breathing either way. Only God has the power to take my breath from me."

She kind of reminds me of an old white version of Violeta except, instead of God, Violeta gives all power to her ancestors. She prays to them, leaves special food for them, lights candles for them, and awaits their guidance. It's the ancestors, according to Violeta, who will have the last word.

Dona Rosa pushes the dish of cookies closer to me and I take a small piece of a broken one. "Did you make these? They're delicious."

"Ai filha, I stopped cooking when I was 85. These are from the store."

I take one more small bite and perch the rest of the broken cookie in my saucer since she didn't make them.

"I used to cook all the time, especially for the festa. I used to make a pecan pie to honor meus pais," she points to the ceiling, then spreads her fingers the way women in my church do when they are particularly pleased with something the pastor is saying or to catch the spirit bouncing off the choir. "My father lived on a pecan farm in Louisiana before his parents came here. He was only four when they left, but he remembered it. It must have been beautiful."

"I don't believe it, Dona Rosa. My father lived on a pecan farm too, in Mississippi. My Grandpa says it was beautiful, too."

Dona Rosa grabs my hand and pushes herself to the edge of her chair, her arm trembling in my grip. "I miss that place like it was my own, filha, like I grew up there, too, but I never laid eyes on it. How can I have saudades for something I never knew?" She rubs a tear from her eye, and then claps her hands together. "What was your farm like?"

I stammer, because I never laid eyes on our farm either, because I too have saudades for a place I never knew. But I can see that she needs something from me, so I try to give it to her. "It was right on the Mississippi Gulf," I say, "and the pecans would fall from the trees." Dona Rosa nods like she can see it, like she knows this make-believe place that I'm talking about. I realize I don't even know what a pecan tree looks like so I tell her one of the stories that Grandpa passed down to me.

"Nobody could believe how far my grandpa could throw a pecan. Grandpa played baseball for the Negro League and he used to catch for Satchel Paige, who according to Grandpa was like the best baseball player ever." I turned down my mouth at this when Grandpa told me because with his bad eyes he couldn't see me do it and because I'd never heard of this Satchel Paige so I didn't see how he could be the greatest anything. I try to describe for Dona Rosa a pecan soaring toward the Gulf of Mexico, skipping through the foamy waves like a rock on a pond.

"The house they lived in was enormous so they used to rent the rooms out to families and the tenant's children liked to cheer my Grandpa on."

They'd see me up front whippin' those pecans, just whippin' 'em so far you couldn't see them land. No sir. Them chillren be runnin' toward the Gulf screamin' 'Mr. Grant done thrown a pecan past the ocean.' That's how Grandpa told the story, but I leave out the slang when I tell it to Dona Rosa.

"So your grandfather was a pecan farmer," Dona Rosa says, "like my grandfather. Did you see my pecan tree?"

I guess I did without realizing it. I guess I had what Violeta is always trying to get at her altar, a talk with my ancestors but I wasn't even trying.

I try to picture Grandpa younger, stronger. He was handsome for sure. I wonder if he would have been Dona Rosa's type, if they'd have gone to a ball game together.

"No, he wasn't a pecan farmer. His grandfather was the pecan farmer. It was his grandfather's plantation. His grandmother was his grandfather's slave."

I've never said these words out loud before and they drop with a thud in the cloaked room, heavy under that suffocating flag. His grandfather, the plantation's owner, didn't have any white children. That's how Grandpa got to live there. The plantation just got passed on to his black heirs when he died.

Grandpa never came right out and told me this. He never said the word "slave." I had to piece it all together from the time period, the place where they lived, that one unit on the Civil War in seventh grade, but mostly from *Roots*. I just worked backwards like *Columbo*.

But I don't tell Dona Rosa this part since she didn't ask, since she's still nodding curiously to make as if she understands but I'm not altogether convinced that she does, so I try to get both our minds to another spot and I make up a lie about how the trees were so dense sometimes kids would get lost playing hide and seek in them and Grandpa'd spend most of his time retrieving frightened children from the property.

"Oh and the house"—now this part is true—"Grandpa said it was beautiful like something in a picture book or in a dream. It was a big old white house with tall shutters and wide windows, only they had to keep those boarded up because of the storms. A long wooden porch ran the length of the front of the house, and the patio off the master bedroom upstairs gave the best view of Ocean Springs. 'Pecan trees everywhere you looked,' Grandpa had said, 'that big ole white house right in the middle of 'em.'"

"Have you been to the house?" Dona Rosa asks.

"No. Our family lost it," I say. Dona Rosa furrows her brow at me and corrects my conjugation.

"How did they lose the house?"

I look into my half empty teacup and let my thumb trace a path around its cool fine edge.

When I asked Grandpa that same question, he sat back and turned his face toward the sun streaming through our kitchen window and hitting the back of his head. He was facing the wrong way if he was looking for Mississippi, but after sitting like that for a long time, the rest of the story seemed to find him. He cleared his throat and took a soiled napkin and patted underneath his glasses.

"I told you I played baseball, didn't I. I could throw a pecan. I could catch a pecan. But I couldn't farm no pecan. Taxes on that big ole place was more than even all them tenants could pay. Your daddy sure did love that house." Grandpa turned away from the sun and got a smile on his face. "But New Orleans, now I got some stories from outta there."

Dona Rosa nods, like she's heard some stories from outta there too. Then, she sits back in her chair. She seems tired. "You really are like my child, you know that? We're from all of the same places." Her eyes still hold a soft green hue despite their age and her skin is still fair even under this penetrating sun. I want to share her belief in our kinship, but it seems unlikely. Even though Grandpa is paler than she is, a shade that would never be confused with morena or even mulatta the way people sometimes call me here, he and I have the same wide forehead, the same accusatory lines across them when we don't believe what we're hearing.

"In that sideboard, in the drawer, there is something for you. Go get it."

I don't move. "Dona Rosa, I can't take anything more from you. I only brought you that pin." I have to search hard to find it, its humble metal overtaken and easily absorbed by all the bold colors and textures of her shawl.

"I didn't plan it, child, but now that I know you, I want you to have this."

Inside the drawer, there is a thick confederate flag with faded colors and yellowing stars unlike any I've seen before. Instead of a red background with a blue cross through the middle, this has a blue square in the left hand corner, like our real flag, and a ring of stars in the square surrounding one bigger star. Then there are three wide stripes, two red and one white. It's sealed up in thick plastic, as precious as The Boy in the Plastic Bubble. I pick it up to look through the rest of the drawer for the present, but only find some books of matches and used candles.

"In your hand. That's it," she says. "Be careful with it and bring it here."

I grip the flag tighter and smile without showing my teeth, so Dona Rosa can't see my anguish and grief.

She holds her hands out and I drop the flag into them like we're playing hot potato. "Cuidado," she says, slowly opening the casing and slipping it out of the sheath. "This thing is older than me."

"That's too valuable, Dona Rosa. Your flag belongs with your family or in a museum."

"There's only me now. No children, not even sobrinhos. But you... I laughed so hard before when you said 'American Brazilian' because that's not a word. We Confederado kids, we're American and Brazilian.

We were brought up speaking English at home, we all went to church together and we were even encouraged to go out together, to hold onto our first home. But I didn't ever feel that place before, not truly, not what it means outside of this place. This flag was the most American thing about me, until today. You made me feel my other country like I never did before. Watch over this for me."

She places the flag in my lap, its heavy tightly woven fibers weighing her arms down, and pets at it like it's a poodle, or John Travolta stuck in his bubble, or a sleeping child. "The cotton in Louisiana was so good. That's why the Portuguese wanted us to come here and bring our cotton seeds with us so they wouldn't have to buy it from the Americans." She sits back in her chair again like she's just seen the end of a pretty dream. "Meus pais always told me that if it weren't for us Americans, this town would have no industry – no Bissacos textile company, no private schools either. The American women started those so their children could receive a proper education." She taps my hand lightly with her own, then lets her hand lay there, like she doesn't have the energy to pick it up again. "You don't see too many of these confederate flags, querida. This was made during the war, before they made that one up there." She points to the window, but I don't look. I feel the same embarrassed rash rising from the collar of my shirt that I get every time Violeta tries to talk to me about "our ancestors" and black solidarity. "Why don't you want my gift, filha?"

I still can't look at her, because I can hear the hurt in her voice. I can hear that she wants to please me as much as I wanted to please her when I first walked through the door. I think of the stupid macaroni necklace my Grandpa gave me, the same day he told me about the pecan farm and how happy I was to have it even though it was ugly. Its ridged shells felt cool and strong between my fingers and I rolled the necklace around for a long time, trying to imagine how Grandpa got the string through the middle, how he dyed the shells all those different shades of green, orange and purple, how they treated him over at the Senior center where he'd made it. "I do want it, Dona Rosa, it's just that…"

"Do you know how many American kids have come through that door, have seen my old flags and clothes and wanted to pry them from my fingers? Never mind the Confederado descendants and the historians."

The one bold ray of light in the parlor has shifted and we are almost in complete darkness except for some cockeyed beams splashing in from the kitchen. The forced blockade of all the light keeps the house nice and cool, but it also casts a heavy shadow on the atmosphere. It's like we're entombed, like there is no way out of here. I sink my fingers into the roots of my hair (I'll need to straighten them soon) and try to figure out something to say.

Chris never has this problem. She just says whatever comes into her half shaved strawberry blonde head and never gets in trouble for it. When that guy at our monthly international club meeting kept "accidentally" grabbing her butt, she had no problem calling him a dirty old pig in front of Jose and some of the other club officers. She hangs loose with her anger, rides it like a wave and doesn't care what anyone thinks. But that never works for me.

Common Sense Rule #11. As an International Exchange Club ambassador, you must at all times behave in a manner which will reflect credit upon you, your family and your country.

"I don't think I could give your gift the proper respect, or the same respect… it doesn't mean the same thing to me, or my family… I don't think my parents would be too happy to have it in their home." I rub my sore shin again even though it's not itching.

"Por que?" Dona Rosa lifts her chin slightly and looks out at me from under her glasses. I hear it now for the first time. The difference between asking "why" and answering "because" is a silence between two syllables. For what. I scratch the back of my ear and picture the blonde guy from the Dukes of Hazzard slipping through the window of that fast orange car of his. I didn't watch it much, because Daisy Dukes' tight jean shorts made me mad and I wanted Bo Duke to come up with something better to say than just Yeehaw. But when I did watch it, I don't recall the big confederate flag painted on the roof of the car bothering me. It only bothered me later, when I was old enough to know that those kinds of things were supposed to bother me, but I can't remember who explained to me the ins and outs of my indignation.

"Dona Rosa, to people in the US a confederate flag means that the person flying it is happy about the confederacy, the way it was before slavery ended." I stroke the flag and try to determine if it's made of cotton or wool, try to remember how I learned that escravo means slave. "It's like saying slavery is a good thing."

She clicks her tongue. "Ai que pena," she says like it's a shame for me that I can't get what she gets from a blue x encrusted with 13 stars on a piece of red cloth. She shifts her weight in her chair and I feel her eyes on me, mine on the big white star in the middle of the 12 littler ones on the itchy flag in my lap. Dona Rosa sticks her yellowing nail into my arm to make me look at her. "What do *you* see when you look at this flag, that I give to you, that my grandfather gave to my father who gave it to me?"

I see myself smacking the glasses off that girl from my old neighborhood a few years before we moved to Akinville because she spent the whole bus ride from school cracking your mama jokes on me and since I didn't want a demerit for fighting, I waited until we were alone on the street and left her groping on the gravel for the broken frames.

I see myself at the Ford Mansion school trip, new to Akinville, without any actual friends yet, going from bedroom to bedroom, the ceilings so low that one girl had to practically bend in half to keep her Jheri curl from brushing against it and I wondered who took care of all those rooms and kept the fires going in each of them at night while Washington and everybody slept. Where did the fire keepers sleep and why didn't the guide mention them? I wanted to know but I did not want to look stupid in front of the other students or "fresh" to the teachers, as my mother had very clearly warned me not to be.

I see myself putting two and two together about my grandfather's grandparents, and why grandpa's skin and my dad's skin were so light even though they were black men. It was sex. Grandpa's grandmother was like Kizzie in *Roots*—the master's sex thing.

I scratch at my sore like crazy now more to make the affection I feel for this woman, rather than my imagined itch go away, and to inspire some stinging hatred to boil up in its place. I mumble, "My parents wouldn't want it in their house."

Dona Rosa chuckles like she just solved a riddle. "Slavery was a good thing, for people who owned slaves, people like my grandfather, but not good for people like your grandfather or his father. Okay. But I'll tell you something, filha, I still want you to have that flag because of what it means to me. When I see this flag, I see our pecan farms. I see what makes us like real family." Dona Rosa yawns.

I should tell her that we're not real family, that I already have a grandfather from the south, and that his pecan farm was swallowed by the stormy gulf, that New Orleans didn't offer promises to him the way Brazil did to her family and that nothing is exactly what he got. Anyway, real family inflicts the realest pain. If Grandpa were here, I think he'd spit on her flag, which makes me doubly mad at myself because I still want to please her.

"You'll come with me to the Campo Cemetery this year when we have our Festa?"

"Claro," I say, trying to hide my repulsion for the flag in my hand, and my excitement at the idea of walking over all of her relatives' graves.

"We'll take some roses from my garden and I'll introduce you to my parents and my grandparents. They're all there."

"It will be my pleasure."

"I'm a little tired now, filha, but come again next Sunday." She takes the flag and tries to put it back in the bag, but doesn't have the dexterity, so she just leaves them both on the coffee table where the tea cups and the cornbread were. "I'll take you to my church, the Baptist church my family started when they came here. Everything was Catholic then." She laughs and closes her eyes. "Everything still is."

I gather up the dishes, bring them to the kitchen and set them on the counter. A pair of garden shears hangs from a nail on the side of the cabinet and I close my eyes and picture my new flag, try and see what it means to me. My mother's angry face staring me down while I dance around the kitchen to Elvis comes to mind. That, and my New Orleans cousins' laughter when I visited them the summer before I entered high school and asked them if we had slaves in our family.

"I'll be happy to go to church with you, Dona Rosa and I'll trim those flowers for you too if you want." But my mangled face in the reflection of the shiny blades doesn't look happy. I look as livid as I felt the day I kicked that girl's ass or on the day I huffed out of the Ford mansion with half a story.

"Just leave the dishes," Dona Rosa calls back. "The maid will be here soon to serve the almoço. She'll clean up." I lick the tip of my finger, dip it into the empty plate of cornbread, then suck down the crumbs until the plate is clean. I can never seem to satisfy the Bissaco's maid, Dona Lucia. She's Italian, like the Bissacos, like a lot of immigrants in this part of São Paulo. No matter how hard I try to pick up after myself and not leave dirty dishes in the sink, I can tell from the way she looks at me that she disapproves of me. I just can't figure out why, if it has to do with my color or my country. I peek out of the kitchen and see Dona Rosa, still with her eyes closed, her hands folded on her lap, flag folded on the table.

"Is it okay if I cut the flowers and bring you some for your coffee table?"

"Next time, when you come for church. We'll do it together."

I return to the parlor just in time to see Dona Rosa in the middle of a moment of clarity that brightens her face. "I think you're right. This flag isn't just mine, it's history, our history. I should share this gift with the people. They've been talking about building an Immigration

Museum…What a fine day we've had," she says.

I wonder what half stories that new museum will tell. I wonder what it would be like to walk around in my grandfather's story all of the time and offer it up to anyone who couldn't understand me. She holds her arms out to me, but I grab them like we're about to do a dozy do so I don't have to feel them around me. I kiss her three times on her cheeks, her skin limp under my lips, and I wonder how hard those loose cheeks would shake if I slapped them, if her lips would quiver if I shook my finger in her face for not giving me the damn flowers, the only things I wanted.

She goes to pat my face again but I back away from her out of her reach, hold my breath so I don't have to smell any lingering cornbread aroma, then grab the flag at the last moment since maybe it will be worth money someday. She calls after me, "Wait, filha, wait. The flag—it's for the museum," and I scream from the other side of the door that I'm late for almoço with my familia verdade.

"De verdade," she screams from behind the screen door, but I don't bother to look back at her or her pecan tree. I don't bother to lift the roses from my path this time and the thorns leave thin gray scratches along my arms. One from a hefty rose near the ground catches on the hem of my jeans. I go to shake it loose, but it's good and snagged so I snap the rose from its tangled bush. I snap a few others loose too and the thorns make a bloody tic-tac toe board on my palm and stain my shirt—another thing that the Bissaco's maid will hold against me.

Tortura. The second entry on my New Portuguese Word list. I knew what it meant the first time I heard it on the news, but like in a dictionary way. I needed to know what it meant for real. So I asked

José one night after dinner, but he said he'd tell me later. When I asked Ana Cásia, she said it was too hard to explain. I didn't bother to ask Claudio because I like the way things are with him and I don't want to do anything to make that change. Only Violeta was straight with me. Only she mentioned the blood, the people no one's ever seen again, the history. I think I'll give her the whole scraggly bouquet. Maybe she'll know what to do with this flag. Or, if she doesn't, maybe the Ancestors will.

I find my dead father at the local supermarket.

Pilar García Guzmán

Apá is the cashier at the store. His face stares back at me.

He rings up bean cans and a soft thud echoes each time he sets one down. He makes sure they're not stacked so that they won't fall. His shriveled fingers tap the worn keyboard, nails wrinkled and bitten.

Apá looks up at me, a slight tilt to his lips that itches my heart. I want to tear it out of my chest and scratch it raw.

"Did you still want the plums?"

The voice is odd. It lacks rasp, it lacks heart. The smile I do recognize. His cheeks and the creases by his eyes remind me of sitting in between his legs, cradled in his arms, while he sat on the couch. I would trace his wrinkles with my pinky, pulling at sags on his skin and thinking that, if I tried hard enough, I would make them go away. Smooth them out and scare them away, if only I scraped my nails against them.

Apá stares at me, expectantly.

"What?" I say.

"There's no price on the plums," he repeats. "Do you remember how much they were?"

This was all wrong.

But his throat. The skin that loosely hangs from his neck and jaw. It's all the same, but the timbre is all wrong. The words are not his own. Apá couldn't speak English. He would try all the time. I would lie on the foot of the bed, my head against his feet and his leg hair tickling my ears. *Only if you teach me,* he would say, *only if you teach me, then I will learn.* I would run to the bag I had dropped by the front door in my rush to get in. The sparkly, green tassels Apá had sewn into it would always get stuck on the zipper. I would pull and tug and rip the thread until it gave, so that I could make my way back to him. And when they were worn enough, he would fix them back up again.

He would fix them after we learned. After I ran with my books and back to the room to teach. As if I had read the words and knew what they all meant, pointing at pictures of a giraffe or a mouse or a whale and sound out the words to him. I would tumble through the vowels with him, and slam against consonants I could not quite pronounce.

Apá would pretend to learn and to know what I was trying to say through words I'd never spoken before. Like how if I had a room in his house I would never have to leave him because the purple walls would be much too pretty and the make-believe bed with lemon colored sheets would grow mold, and dust, if there wasn't someone to sleep in it every night. But he didn't understand because those were words my mouth could never shape quite right.

We would both speak and try to understand. Our tongues a mess.

But Apá would nod along, and I would nod along, listening to the nothingness, the willingness, between us. No real words, but a real memory.

So I know I have it all wrong.

Except his cheeks and his nose.

"Miss?"

I shake my head, force myself to look away. My shoelaces are untied, the aglets muddy.

"Yes?"

"Would you like me to check for you?" he asked.

"What?"

"The plums."

"Oh. No."

"No?"

"I don't want them."

Apá throws the bag on the belt next to him, doesn't look at it again. The bag topples over, two plums tumble out and stop by his feet. He kicks them out of the way, scans the rest of the things I put on the belt.

On his wrist, a digital watch blinks big, blocky numbers on the screen.

The luminescent orange band makes his skin look yellowish, and his veins protrude in jagged zig zags from the back of his hand.

I grab the bags, make myself hold on to them, and head to the door. When I look back at Apá, he's frowning at the next customer in line with two loaded carts of bright green sponges and translucent detergent.

I go outside, put the bags in my car, and go back inside.

* * *

The last people in line stuff boxes of chocolate bars and flavored caramel and cherry and mint into a single plastic bag. They chat softly about an office debacle and losing a bet. Apá listens eagerly, throwing his head back with a chuckle.

A heave and jumping ribs strain through the thin fabric of his shirt. I know that wheezing, that sort of breathlessness.

Apá and I would sit on the porch of his house during my visits, staring out at the street as cars passed by. I wasn't allowed to see him often, but a few times per month Apá was all mine. One whole day at a time.

He would rock back and forth in an iron rocking chair that squeaked and croaked. One day, I ran over to the garden hose and filled up my small, plastic cup with water. The kind of cup that would wrinkle with use when I fisted it tight, ones we only used to throw out. The water sloshed over the rim, so I moved carefully and poured it on the creases of the chair where the metal had gone brittle and brown. Back and forth,

I went and I poured water on the chair until it all pooled beneath it. I sat beside it, ignoring the water slowly soaking my pants, and scooped up as much as I could in my hands. I poured it on Apá's knees, letting it trickle through my fingers and along his skin.

He looked down at me. *What are you doing?*

Oiling your joints, I said.

And he laughed, scooping me up from the ground and holding me on his lap, against his chest.

His lungs strained in his chest, blown up like balloons, and what if they popped? I thought they might pop and then he might die. What if he died because of the wheezing in his throat? Because of the air that refused to leave his lungs? Because they would grow much too big and wide, until they popped? I could see his heart hammering away through his skin. I hugged him tight and pressed my face, my lips, to his chest, hoping I could breathe air into him and maybe that could keep his laugh alive.

But he is not Apá.

Not Apá smiles at the customer, hands them a receipt and turns to look at me.

"Forget something?" he asks.

I set a new basket on the belt, fold my hands behind my back, and Not Apá loses his smile. His hair stands out straight at his neck like spikes on a collar. I want to reach out and prick my finger on them, in case they're also fake.

Not Apá pulls out the items: a set of multicolored scrunchies, a box of double dipped Oreos, two bags of jumbo cotton balls, and a set of butcher knives.

He looks at me as he bags them up, tilting the screen to show me the total. He clears his throat. "Cash or card?"

Not Apá fists the bag in his hand, not yet giving it to me. The band on his watch is so big on his wrist that it dances up and down as he moves.

I glance at the total. "The knives are on sale." I lie.

"You sure?"

I nod.

He looks at me, then at the screen. His knuckles whiten as they grip my bag harder. "I'll get one of the managers for you then."

"No."

"No?"

"No need to bother anyone. I'll just take them."

"Well then, cash or card?" Not Apá's mouth pinches tight. He extends his free hand towards me. Close enough to clutch at my shirt, in case I run away, I guess.

Not Apá wears a brown, knitted vest over a yellow shirt. On top, a blue, wrinkled flannel with all the buttons undone and a stain on the left pocket. His clothes swish around his body in bundles of excess fabric.

Apá had a big belly, and his clothes were always littered with stretch marks that mirrored the ones along his back. I wonder what it would be like to clutch Not Apá's clothes in a fist and twist them around my hand. If I pulled at them tight enough, the vest and the shirt and the layered flannel might all stick to his body like a second skin, and maybe then he would just be Apá.

I look at his outstretched hand, the bitten nails.

"Your watch is broken," I say.

Not Apá looks up. "What?"

"Broken."

"Oh, I hadn't noticed. I guess it is."

I open my bag, pretending to look for something. Then I pretend to not find something, so that he'll speak again. And maybe it'll be Apá who speaks instead, a garbled tongue and mismatched speech.

"Miss, either pay or leave," Not Apá says.

"Huh?"

"Do you want your things?"

"Yes, I'm just finding my wallet."

"There's still no sale. Is that ok?"

"Yes, that's fine."

"Great, it'll be–"

"What about your watch though?" I interrupt.

People behind me mutter, impatient words graze the back of my neck. Not Apá won't stop staring at me, and I wish I could stay here, staring back.

"Miss, you're holding up the line," he says.

The clock on Apá's wall was so loud that he never looked at it to know what time it was. But I did. The golden hands swished behind the glass much too fast. I hoped that if I stared at them long enough, I could stop them. But Apá would tap my hand so that I focused on the carrots and the knife. The dining room chairs were so old that the springs would cut into the back of my thighs and the marks would stay there for days, even after I'd left. Sometimes, I thought they did it on purpose, to keep me there. A reminder of what it was like, so I'd never forget being there.

We would sit, and Apá would sing *un letargo de azul, un eclipse the mar,* and I didn't understand. I never really understood what that meant and I never thought to ask. Peeling carrots and potatoes and yuca to store in the freezer, I barely had time to ask. Then Apá would defrost food we had prepped during prior visits, and he would cook and serve it for me to eat. The springs beneath the chair's cushion gripping me in place.

Never strong enough for me to stay.

I would look back at the clock again, scared.

"What's your name?" I ask Not Apá.

He sighs, and that's the closest his lungs have come to sound like Apá's. Still holding my bag, he points to a name tag propped next to the keyboard.

Howard.

I never met a *Howard* before.

* * *

Howard leaves the store hours later. He shuffles along the sidewalk towards a car parked around the curb. His thin legs move his body along in tiny steps, exhaustion weighing him down. From my car, I see a blanket of rain around him that dampens his clothes.

My body moves on its own. I jerk the car door open and run across the parking lot. Howard doesn't notice me until I'm a foot away. His eyes go wide, his arms jut out, and I wrap my arms around him. Swallow him whole in a hug he doesn't return.

His body tenses, and the aged muscles of his arms bunch up. I can feel Apá's papada against my shoulder, rubbing against my ear, and his warm, heavy breath at my neck. His lungs wheeze from years smoking cheap cigarettes and borrowed cigarros. And so his hair—thin as only gray hair can be—smells like tobacco too.

I hide my face in his shoulder and watch as my tears soak his vest, already wet from the rain.

He is tiny against me—wiry, brittle bones I don't quite recognize. He stands with his arms against his body, and he won't look at me. I want him to look at me because he might recognize my shoes or my watch or the tassels on my backpack.

Maybe he would remember me if I still wore my purple tights, smeared with paint, and the corduroy hat that hid my lopsided pigtails. Then his face would split open in a smile, his crooked, gapped teeth projecting joy across the parking lot.

I wish he would close his eyes and bury his face in my neck.

Apá embroidered stars along the rim of my hat in every single color thread he could afford to buy. When it was done, he slapped it on my head and I could barely see from beneath it.

I left it somewhere in his house after my last visit.

Living in America
Zabe Bent

Daddy wasn hearing me, or maybe he wasn listening, so I just came out and said it: "I don't want to go to Jamaica again."

He puffed out some smoke, no clean rings, just renk cigarette clouds. He'd been puffing my whole life, and I still didn understand how he could smoke in this finger-freezin weather. "How yuh mean, yuh don' want to go Jamaica again?" he said.

The school bleachers felt cold against my bottom, but Mummy still made me wear long johns under my band uniform and they took off most of the chill. I was old enough to come to games on my own, but Grandma gave me a ride and Daddy was supposed to meet us. Minutes before halftime and he just got here, even though everybody else who came on the train from Grand Central was here long ago. I should've been on the field but he waved me over to the bleachers when he came. Coach said it was okay because we were only waiting, waiting for the whistle to blow, waiting for the band to go on. Daddy leaned forward, with his elbows on his knees. His face was well close to mine but he wasn looking at me. Which is good, because I didn really want to see his face squinge up again. And I meant "again" in the American way, as in "not another time," rather than the Jamaican way, as in "not any more." Not any more is how I felt about spending the summer in Jamaica. But

Daddy didn get it.

"I don't want to go," I said. I bit out every word carefully, to make sure I was clear. "My friends are all going camping. In the woods. Everyone's already talking about it." My knee was bouncing, and I didn notice until he put his hand over my knee.

Daddy moved his hand soon as the tiktik noise of my shoelaces against the bleachers stopped. "Is what? Two years now since you don' go home? Junior, yuh don' miss it?"

I didn answer. Grandma pulled on my baseball cap, like she always did. It'd probably get annoying one day, but grandmas are grandmas. "Yuh didn have a good time at my house that summer?" she said.

"Yuh didn like runnin round with yuh cousins and yuh friends from before?" Daddy said, "With Denton and Dwayne and Sekou and alla dem from yuh old school?"

"I have friends here too, Daddy." I said. "Friends I only get to see at camp."

"Yuh don' want to get away from New York for awhile?" he said.

Daddy always needed a break, always wanted to get away from here. He was always looking back to Jamaica. I think, to Daddy, New York was everything up here. Not just The City but all the barbecues at Bear Mountain was New York and all the visits to Wilson's Woods pool was New York just as much as the Statue of Liberty and the Empire State Building and all the field trips Mummy chaperoned for us was New York. But to me, "Going camping upstate is not New York, Daddy, not

New York City anyway. Up there is not like here, where we can walk five minutes to the station, jump on Metro North, and half-hour later we're in Midtown. Camp is five hours upstate. Really upstate, not just Westchester. And we go deep into the woods. We hike for at least an hour, then we get to sleep outside and swim in the lake and go fishing and build fires and pick fruit in the middle of nowhere."

The tiktik noise of shoelaces on metal came back, but it wasn me this time. I checked. Daddy said, "Yuh can pick fruit and build fires at your aunt's house back home, in country. Yuh don' remember how her cherry trees nice? Yuh didn like seeing yuh family and yuh friend dem and eatin off all the hardo bread and patties and ice cream and all that?" He always tried to convince me with food. Abi even joked that I would be Jamaican-In-Food-Only if I kept up the trend. Usually food bribes worked. Not this time.

"Abi can bring back some for me, right?" I said. I was looking at him now. He was still looking into the crowd. "Probably not the cherries. I don't think they let us bring in cherries, even if they're picked and frozen like Auntie does when she sends up ackee. I never understood that. Ackee's poisonous."

"Only if yuh don' know how to manage it," Grandma said. "These people can be so silly, nuh so?"

"They are really silly," I said.

"Just can't let people be happy," Dad said.

I smiled, as wide as I could. Puppy dog eyes wouldn work, partly because dogs were outside animals to my Jamaican dad, not fluffy cutesy things that white people let lick off their dinner plates before they put them into dishwashers we didn have. But also because Dad would tell me I was too old for "dat sort o foolishness." Not just getting old, fully too old now, because I'd be in high school soon. So I smiled some more and nudged my shoulder into his. "Will you let me be happy, Dad? Come on, just let me go camping again. We'll do this year just like last year? You know you want to?"

He cracked a smile this time, same like mine, only a little smaller. For now. I knew we could get him there, if I worked him a little longer. He took another puff, blew it out, then smashed the stub on the bleacher seat.

"Yuh modda and I have to discuss it. But Junior, wi decide from longtime that yuh would travel wid Abi dis summer. From last year she have wi under heavy manners to save for it."

"You can use the money to pay for camp. The deposit is due next week. Just the deposit, Daddy, to reserve my spot." I pause. "Abi's been old enough to travel on her own for awhile now," I said, as if he didn already know. "And you know Mummy will say no."

"Then is no," Daddy said. "Why yuh bodda ask mi?"

"You're the one who called me over here. You're the one who wanted to talk. Come mek wi reason', you said."

"So yuh tell mi, too," Grandma said. "Is why I came this way before work."

Dad's eyebrows went up. He tapped his fingers against his pack of

Dunhills. "Well," he said, "I did have something else to talk bout, but now I have to sort out how to talk to yuh daughter-in-law bout this likkle ting."

"Mi nuh tink it so likkle. And dem sorta details is between you and she," Grandma said. "I don' know that is a good idea for me to get involved in business between man and wife."

"Now yuh decide yuh don' want get involve? Now, when I ask yuh to involve yuhself?" Daddy cut his eye at Grandma, and she actually let him get away with it.

My mouth dropped open and she cut her eye back at him, and said, "He's only joking, Junior. Mostly. I soon leave, though."

Daddy checked his watch and looked across the field, then into the parking lot, and back at his watch again. "Yuh not goin to stay longer, Mama? I invite somebody here to meet yuh. To meet the two o yuh."

I knew there had to be a reason Daddy came. Sometimes he would get away from work to watch my soccer matches, but this was only the third or fourth time he came to see me march. I should have known something was up when he asked for me, instead of just waiting until after the game to take me home.

"Somebody for me to meet? Here? Now?" Grandma stared at Daddy, so long it made my skin creep. Then she looked at her wrist watch and said, "I don' think so. I have to go work."

Dad slapped his Dunhills against his palm. The slim, red and gold box bounced into his handmiddle a few times, til it slowed to a rhythm, like he was counting off points inside his head. Everything changed about his body language, and in a bland English he rarely spoke outside the few PTA meetings we went to, he said, "Mama, I would really like the both of you to stay and meet mi friend. She soon reach. She's just in the car park."

Grandma's hands went to her hips. She looked bigger somehow, strong and soft and hard and soft again at the same time. I'd never thought about her being soft or hard or anything at all, because she gave such comfy hugs. But this was not that. From the flat look on her face, I could tell two things: (1) that she had absolutely no desire to meet any of Dad's "new friends" and (2) that I probably didn want to meet them either. Not these friends. Not the ones he set up for us to meet here, or anywhere anytime when Mummy would not be coming. And (3) that she didn want to talk about it anymore. It almost felt like she wanted to say these things to him too. At least some of them. Instead she just said, "Mi neva teach yuh better dan dis?"

"Mama," he said, but he didn say anything else. He just looked at her, his lips pushing in, out, and around his whole face, like his thoughts were trying to come out but knew better. When I looked at Grandma, her lips were as still and thin as the hands on her hips.

I felt squirmy in between them staring at each other so long, so I changed the subject. "Are we settled on camp, Dad?" I asked. "Can I go?"

"Maybe I could let it pass. Your mother now… your mother had plans for you this summer. She wanted you to stay with her sister this time," Daddy told me. "Your cousins wanted to take you to country and—"

Grandma jumped in again, "And nearly split his fore'ead in half trying to open coconut with machete?"

"Don' remind me," Dad said to her, but his tone was all joke. I could have laughed with him, but he wasn there with us. That memory was right below the surface, close enough that I remembered how scary it was. It frightened me to watch the dull but very narrow end of a machete nearly ram into Abi's big forehead when she yanked it, too hard, after she'd wedged it into the big ol coconut. Also frightening to have to explain to Daddy and Mummy both that I'd failed to protect my sister from death or dismemberment. Like I was her keeper or something, just because I was the oldest, even though I was only a ten year old city kid hangin out in country, much less in a place I barely knew anymore. She had a thin scar on her forehead that didn need stitches. The doctors said it would heal into a teeny tiny line no one would notice. Eventually.

"We could tell Mummy I'll see everyone when they come to visit," I said. I didn want to let this drop. Partly because I didn want to talk about his new friend, and partly because it felt like I absolutely had to come away from this discussion knowing where I'd spend summer, knowing it wouldn be in Jamaica. "I'll promise not to complain, even if she doesn let me bring any comic books to read while we're there."

"You know she won' give yuh extra credit for doing what you're already supposed to do," Dad said, "like not complain when we visit family. Family sent any and every thing they could when we came here, same like yuh aunties who took us in and always mek sure we understand how to get you and yuh sister into good school and mek sure we have somewhere to eat and dance come holiday time."

"So don't say, I'll see em when they get here." I said. "Got it. Got it."

Dad nudged my shoulder with his forearm. "Y'know, sometime yuh really favor me. Yuh just try a ting and tek it as it come." I wasn sure that was the compliment, or if even he thought it was.

"Dat is my cue. Wi can talk lata, y'hear, son?" Grandma said to Daddy. "And good luck to you, Junior. Just speak your heart, you can manage. You can get through." She stood up, tied her jacket belt round her belly, and headed to the parking lot. Each step she took, I wanted it to be in the other direction, back to help me explain things to Daddy.

The noise of a jet engine roared, distant and high above us. The football game went on, classmates and families cheering as one of the teams msde a touchdown. I didn even know if it was my team. I didn care, but staring into the parking lot gave me an idea. I just had to work up to it. I put it in my back pocket for safe keeping, and hoped it stayed there.

"We could remind Mummy that I don't like to fly," I said. "She hates pumping us full of drugs, and I'm definitely not getting on a plane again without Dramamine. Two doses. Each way. First thing she'll say is, 'you realize how much that cost?'"

Dad chuckled into the ground below the risers. He took a minute to breathe, then he finally looked at me. It was always strange to look at someone who looked like looking into the mirror, but was so clearly not me. His afro was gone, just low low now, like I had to wear my hair for school, especially with the hat for the band uniform. But he was still sporting a beard and I couldn even grow a mustache yet. He passed his hand over the beard now, tightening fingers around his chin. "Is it really the flying though, Junior? I know yuh don' like it, but I just feel is something else."

TikTikTikTikTikTik. My eyes found the ground. It felt so so far away, and so so close, like I was falling into a swirling pool of grass and metal and asphalt. Like when we were at the top of the Empire State for that school trip with Mummy, looking down on the big buildings and tiny cars and ant-people.

"Yuh don' have to, but if yuh want to tell me is what, Junior, yuh can?"

"But it's true, Dad, I really don't like flying." After a moment, I added, "I'm not trying to lie to Mummy."

Dad angled his head to stare at me from his eyecorner. "Okay, son. If yuh seh so." He put his hand on my knee again, waited for me to quiet down, and said, "But is a short flight. And is not like you can drive go home. So talk to mi. Talk di truth."

TikTikTikTikTikTik.TikTikTikTikTikTik.

"I won't want to come back." Even I could hear how soft my voice was. I suppose that's why Dad didn say anything. Not at first.

A bold buzz drowned out the sounds of the football game in front of us and swallowed up the noise of the crowd. When Daddy spoke, his voice was so low and so soft, as though he was really and truly trying to understand, like deep water tumbling in and out of river rocks til they come smooth. "Junior. Yuh just tell me that yuh don' want to go at all. How yuh mean yuh don' want to come back?"

TikTikTikTikTikTik. TikTikTikTikTikTik. TikTikTikTikTikTik.

My knee was bouncing. I think the whole of the bleachers were moving.

I didn know how to say the next words. I didn know how to tell him what he should already know. Grandma had sorted it out months ago, or weeks at least. She said I should try to be happy. Or at least try not to hold everything inside til it hurt.

"Junior," Dad said, "just tell me. I won' get vex this time."

"Dad, don't you remember how they wouldn let me in last time?"

"Of course they let you in. If they didn let you in, yuh wouldn be here now."

"I didn' say didn't. I said wouldn't." But I could see understanding dawn in his eyes. A sparkle was there, just not the playful look he got, the one that settled in his eyecorner when we joked around.

"Yuh mean, at the airport, don't it?" he said, and I nodded.

Dad's eyelids drooped, seemed to hang even lower than his nose. "But we were there, Junior. We were there with you."

My whole body snapped forward, turned to him, still and rigid. "Not at first, Dad. Not for hours. All because of my skin."

He clutched at his beard again. "Well, not really because of your skin, not like dat," he said. I rolled my eyes. "Because of the mosquito bites on your skin, Junior. You had so many, and yuh had calamine lotion all over yuh."

"You'd think they'd never seen anyone with mosquito bites before," I said.

"They thought you were carrying in measles, Junior. Your mother only had to show them your vaccination papers and then they released you. It just took a little while for her to find the right people, for us to connect to dem."

"No, Dad. It wasn just the measles. They thought my papers were wrong. That's why. They thought my papers were fake."

"How yuh mean fake? Yuh never tell me that."

"They didn believe I was just a kid. They thought I was sixteen. Because I'm so tall. So if the papers could lie and say I was twelve, then they must be fake. That's what they kept saying, that my papers were fake and I was illegal and I didn belong. Right up until you and Mummy came into the room."

Daddy didn say a word. He just sat with his hands on the bleacher seats, knuckles tight and bright.

"They put me in a room, by myself, for that whole time. I think they let Abi sit outside, but she was by herself too. For hours, Daddy."

"Come now, Junior. It was hours but maybe only bout two. Two hours is not so long." He was silent for a moment or longer. "That's why you don' want to fly home again?"

Tik Tik Tik Tik Tik Tik. Tik Tik Tik Tik Tik Tik. Tik Tik Tik Tik Tik Tik.

"They asked a lot of questions. Big, grown men in dark uniforms. They searched our bags. They opened all the food Auntie wrapped up in foil and stuck their noses so deep in it til I don't even want to eat fry fish and bammy anymore."

Dad didn say anything then. Neither of us were fidgeting either. Just sitting, listening to the sounds of gameplay. I wished the half-time whistle would blow so I could grab my trumpet and line up to take the field.

"They don't give you anything to do, Dad. I was twelve, so Abi was what, ten? They wouldn let either of us watch their television. Or listen to their radio. We had those playing cards from the stewardess, but they made me leave them on the table. No books. Not even paper and pencil to draw or doodle. Just stare at the wall in that white room. For hours. While they ask questions about every little thing they're rifling through. Over and over again. They probably memorized all the colors of my underpants. You think I want to go through that again? Ever?"

"We got through as quickly as we could, son. We had our papers and yours, and we were calling everyone's name, everyone I know at airport and everyone yuh Auntie know too. We got through to you as quickly as we could." He looked up, and I wondered if there were tears filling his eyes, threatening to spill over the edges like pool water. I don't know why, but as far as I could remember, he always looked up to cry. He leveled off and said, "Son, that was years ago. Don't let it get to you. Don't let that be the reason you don't go home again."

I tried to come up with other options, racked my brain trying to think of something more, anything, but it felt like I was fumbling and flailing and falling falling falling. He kept looking around the parking lot, and I kept hoping I wouldn have to pull anything from my pocket. I couldn play dominoes like he could, but I knew a trump when I had one. How do I make him understand that it wasn just then? That it was always there for me, and for Abi too? Wasn it like that for them too? Something old or new every single day?

"Do you remember when Abi went to Montreal or Quebec or wherever for French class?" I said.

We sat there a minute, until he realized I was waiting for him to nod.

"The whole group drove up there on a bus," I said. "It was sixty kids and a few teachers. When they got to the Canadian border, their bus had to pull over. The teachers said the border agents would have to interview anyone who wasn a US citizen. All the green card kids got pulled off the bus and taken to some tiny shoebox office. Like one of those overflow container joints they have in crowded schools and hospitals? It was Abi and two or three other kids. A couple of them were were refugees, from Yugoslavia and Ethiopia or somewhere. Their teacher said, either way, they'd just stamp their passports and let them go. But they could have done that from the bus. Abi said they questioned all of them for an hour. She's gotta be wrong on that, that seems so long. But it must have felt that way to her, as a kid."

"The teachers would have done something," Dad said. "All o them a citizen. Dem coulda step in. Dem woulda move things along."

"Yeah, well, maybe they didn think sitting for an hour was that long." I was trying to keep calm, but I felt my heart jumping into my ribs and sweat coating my fingers. I heard blood rushing in my ears too. "Anyway, I guess it felt like hours to Abi. Whatever. The point is that the whole bus had to wait for them. While border agents questioned three eleven- or twelve-year-old kids. They were coming back from a class trip. It should have just been a fun ten-hour bus ride, if that's a thing. She said it felt like that time at the airport all over again, because she didn't really know what the border agents were looking for or if they were going to harass her or her friends or what. And when the three of them got back on the bus, the other kids, the Americans, they needled them about it half-way back to the schoolyard. She said those kids, supposedly her friends, asked if they were smuggling things into the country. Just like when we first came, when people used to ask if we came over on a dinghy, instead of Air Jamaica. They didn't get how freaked out she was, or they were, they just kept making jokes."

TikTikTikTikTikTikTik. "She never told me about that, Junior. I don't think she told your mother either." Dad was staring into the field, long and hard, like he would rather let it swallow him than talk about this.

"What could you have done?" I asked. I sat on my hands, trying to keep them still. "Abi and me, we see you guys working hard. Trying. I know it doesn't seem like it but we do. We never want to bring you something where you couldn't do anything, or worse, where you would want to do something really bad instead."

"I am the Daddy," he said. "Yuh supposed to bring these things to me. To us. We are the parents. We are the ones to sort out these things."

"It just seems like this is how it is here, Dad. It's just how things work."

"Then if yuh know that, yuh must know that sometimes, is so it go."

"That doesn't mean I have to like it."

"No," he said. "Seem like yuh want to choose it, though." This time, Dad didn't bother to look into the sky, and I wished I could just leave already. He started packing the Dunhills again, and I hoped he waited for me to leave to spark up. I saw his tears, ready to drop out, and I hoped they waited for me to leave too. "Abi still goes home. She went last year fall. That was after the bus trip."

"You mean for GranGran's funeral?" Everyone knew GranGran was one of Abi's favorites. She'd probably scale the Chrysler Building for her, or at least the clock tower at school, and Abi was afraid of heights.

"Right," Dad said. I think maybe it was fitting together. "But you neva go dat time."

"I got lucky," I said, staring at the field, noting that my bandmates were starting to line up. "Mummy said we could only afford two tickets. And obviously it wasn going to be you and her, and leave us kids alone. Grandma had to work. And so did Aunt Vi. And pretty much everyone else. So it had to be one of us and one of you. I got lucky."

He blanched at that. "Junior, these things happen."

"Okay, Dad."

"It worked itself out. You can manage."

"I have enough to manage here."

"Don't let that keep you away from home."

"Dad, I don't want to go," I said, "And Mummy wouldn make me."

I followed Dad's glance to the parking lot and saw an unfamiliar face there. When I looked at Dad I saw an unfamiliar smile, one he hadn't shared with us. I got up, pulled my cap down, snuggled into my jacket, and started down the bleachers.

"Wi not finished, Junior. Where yuh goin?" Dad looked in my direction but it felt like his eyes went behind me, to the parking lot. Peering over his glasses and underneath his breath he said, "Don't be rude. Yuh modda raise yuh betta dan dat."

"…My mother?" It was hard not to yell it at him, but I thought of everyone's eyes turning our way, seeing everything unfold. I rolled my shoulders, reset. I sat up straight and tall like Mummy taught me, like Grandma always told me. Then I told Dad, "Don't force me to do things I don't want to do. Don't make me say things I shouldn't have to say either."

His eyes flicked behind me and back to me again. "Mind yuhself."

I could feel the energy of the field around me. The chatter of the teams leaving the field, debriefing the first half. The woodwinds playing a note here and there while the horn section warmed up. I should be with them, and I wondered whether it was their eyes I felt on me or someone else's. It wasn't Dad. No, his eyes moved between me, the woman approaching from the parking lot, and the field. I waited for him to say something, say anything, but he just stared at me, the skin under his left eye twitch twitching like it could flick out at me.

"The deposit is due next week," I said.

"I don't know yet, Junior. How much is it exactly?"

"The deposit secures my spot. And it's way less than the plane ticket," I said.

"Deposit for what?" She was here now, the unfamiliar face from the parking lot. That new friend of his, a tall, thin, brown-to-pale woman with dark hair down her back. She looked just like Mummy and nothing like her at all. I told myself I didn care bout that, didn care bout any of it. But I found myself standing, first on one foot then the other, then back to the first again.

I think they thought I stood to greet her, that I was nervous to meet her or something. I glanced at Dad.

"This is my big son. Junior, we call him." He turned to me, saying, "This is Carmen."

She extended her hand to me. It felt like the music stopped, like everyone from the field fixed their eyes on the three of us. "It's nice to meet you," she said, and sound flooded my ears, as if the crowd itself was the mouth of the largest horn section I'd ever heard. I fought to focus. I glanced at Dad, right hand creeping out of my pocket, ready but resting.

My hand hovered in the air between us, between me and this woman, as I focused on Dad. "I'm sorry, but I really have to go."

"You're leaving so soon?" she asked.

"Yes, he has to go down to the field," Dad said, nodding at me with a slump in his shoulders and ice in his eyes.

"Good to meet you, I guess." I shoved my hand back into my pocket. My shoulders slumped even more than Dad's, like they could finally shrink from the tension they'd been gripping. "I'll get those details to you, Dad."

I turned back to the field and started walking.

I don' know what Dad said next, or maybe I just didn care. I also didn care how he reacted to my decision, because I wasn asking how to get out of going anymore. I don' know how he planned to tell Mummy and Abi and everybody else that I was not going to Jamaica this summer or any other. All I heard was the tiktiktiktiktiktiktik again, when I got past the risers. I turned back to see how he looked, to see if he was facing the sky or facing the field or chatting up his new friend. I told myself I didn care bout that either, so long as I wasn there, wasn a part of any of it. By the time the whistle blew, I was already on the field, lining up with the band.

Contributor Bios

alphabetical by first

Aimee R. Cervenka is a writer, climate activist, and professional baker. Her poetry has appeared or is forthcoming in more than a dozen publications, including *Poet Lore, Ascent,* and *Slab,* and was a finalist in *Iron Horse Literary Review's* 2023 PhotoFinish. Her micro-collection "(Not Quite) Political Animals" was published in March 2023 by Rinky Dink Press. She lives in Spokane, Washington.

Alba Delia Hernández is an award winning writer, inspired by Puerto Rico, growing up in Bushwick, and salsa, who dances in the hybrid forms of fiction, playwriting and poetry. She was a featured reader for The Bushwick Starr's 2023 Reading Series and was awarded the winner of the 2022 One Festival for her one woman show, Juana Peña Revisited. She is a recipient of the Creatives Rebuild New York (CRNY) Award, the Bronx Council on the Arts First Chapter Award and earned a Bachelor of Arts degree from Columbia University. Her writing was highly commended in A Gathering of the Tribes Magazine, El Proyecto de La Literatura Puertorriqueña through the University of Houston's USLDH and the Mellon Foundation, and other publications. She has performed at El Museo del Barrio, The Whitney Museum, Nuyorican Poets Café, La Respuesta in Puerto Rico and other venues. She's a passionate yoga teacher, salsa dancer, and videographer who recites speeches by Puerto Rican revolutionaries or moves to songs of resistance.

Anna Kreienberg is a student who lives and works in Pittsburgh, PA. She can be reached at a.kreienberg@gmail.com

Cleyvis Natera is a novelist, short story writer, essayist, and critic. She is the author of the debut novel *Neruda on the Park,* which was a New York Times Editor's Choice and was awarded a Silver Medal by the International Latino Book Awards for Best First Book of Fiction. The recipient of awards and fellowships from PEN America, the Vermont Studio Center, Hermitage Artist Retreat, and Bread Loaf Writers' Conference, Natera studied literature and creative writing at Skidmore College and holds a M.F.A. in Fiction from New York University. Her fiction, essays and criticisms have appeared in *Kirkus, The New York Times Book Review, URSA, TIME, Gagosian Quarterly, The Brooklyn Rail, The Rumpus, The Washington Post, Pleiades, The Kenyon Review, Aster(ix)* and *Kweli Journal,* among others. Her second novel, The *Grand Paloma Resort,* is forthcoming August 2025 from Ballantine Books. Natera currently teaches creative writing at Barnard College of Columbia University and Montclair State University. At Montclair State University, Natera leads the development of a new Bilingual M.F.A. Creative Writing Program.

Cristina Herrera Mezgravis is a writer and educator from Valencia, Venezuela. She graduated from Stanford University with awards in both fiction and nonfiction. She worked in tech and in college prep in the Bay Area and in Lima, Peru. She currently lives in Austin, Texas with her husband and their tabby cat, Lima. As a second-year MFA candidate at the Michener Center for Writers, Cristina is working on a coming-of-age novel about Venezuelan migrants.

Dionne Ford is author of *Go Back and Get It,* a 2024 finalist for the Hurston/Wright Award in memoir. She is also co-editor of the anthology *Slavery's Descendants: Shared legacies of Race and Reconciliation.* Her work has won awards from the National Endowment for the Arts, the National Association of Black Journalists and the Newswomen's Club of New York. Dionne holds an MFA in fiction from NYU and a BA from Fordham University where she teaches creative writing.

Ellen Hagan is a writer, performer, and educator. Her books include: *Crowned, Hemisphere, Watch Us Rise* (YA collaboration with Renée Watson), *Blooming Fiascoes, Reckless, Glorious, Girl, Don't Call Me a Hurricane, All That Shines and Tell Me Every Lie* (YA collaboration with David Flores forthcoming from Bloomsbury, Spring 2025). Ellen's poems and essays can be found in: *So We Can Know: Writers of Color on Pregnancy, Loss, Abortion, and Birth, Creative Nonfiction, Underwired Magazine, She Walks in Beauty, Small Batch, Southern Sin,* ESPNW and Oprah Daily. www.ellenhagan.com @ellenhagan

Frankie Ochoa's short stories have appeared in *La Presa, Nat. Brut, Kweli Journal, The Account,* and elsewhere. Her short story "Still Life" received a notable mention in the 2018 Pushcart Prize Anthology, and is anthologized in *Aster(ix) 10th Anniversary Issue* (Blue Sketch Press). She is currently working on her debut novel, *Citizen of Memory.* The novel follows Nina Miller who works for the Memory Seekers, an organization dedicated to reuniting families torn apart by kidnappings and fraudulent adoptions that took place during El Salvador's civil war. An adoptee herself, raised by lesbian parents in the Bay Area, Nina has always been devoted to the work. But when she discovers a DNA match that identifies her friend Violeta's long-lost sister, the mission becomes deeply personal. Determined to bring the sisters together after nearly forty years, Nina follows the trail to the U.S.-Mexico border, where a new crisis of missing children is unfolding. As she unearths the past, Nina is forced to confront the complexities of memory, identity, and history's enduring hold on the present.

Leo D. Martinez is an Afro-Dominican American artist from Harlem, NY, who resides in Atlanta, GA. A Periplus fellow, she has published her fiction in *Plantin Magazine* and *¡Pájaros, lesbianas y queers, a volar! Anthology* and her non-fiction in *Electric Literature;* she was also an honorable mention for the 2021 BCLF Elizabeth Nunez Award for Caribbean-American Writers. You can find her napping on a rock by a river, walking her dog, or on Instagram & Twitter @leyetheecreator.

A lover of words and their meanings across languages, **Kleaver Cruz** (they/them) was born and raised in Uptown, NYC between The Bronx and Washington Heights with their twin and small Dominican family. Kleaver is a Black queer writer, educator and artist that is deeply interested in the crevices of archives and history. Their work is the marriage between curiosity of what has come before and the creative imagining of what can be; there's an insistence on creating mirrors and clearing up the ones already there. They have presented and conducted work across the African Diaspora and continent in places like Brazil, South Africa and The Netherlands, among other countries. Kleaver is the Facilitator of The Black Joy Project, a digital and real-world affirmation that Black joy is resistance. Kleaver is a 2024 nominee for the NAACP Image Award for Outstanding Debut Author. They are the author of *The Black Joy Project: A Literary and Visual Love Letter to How We Thrive.* (Mariner Books/HarperCollins). Kleaver believes in the power of words to write the stories that did not exist when they needed them the most.

Naima Ramos-Chapman tells stories of transformation and understated bravery by rendering the juxtaposition of psycho-spiritual realities we can not see alongside the normalized brutalities "hiding" in everyday life. Their first short, AND NOTHING HAPPENED, explored the psychological aftermath of a sexual assault and premiered at the 2016 Slamdance Film Festival. Their second short, PIU PIU, a meditation on frontier justice and victimhood ontology, premiered at Slam Dance Festival in 2018. Also in 2018, they wrote, directed, acted in, and edited the season finale for the Peabody award-winning *Random Acts of Flyness* (HBO). In 2020, as part of a multi-media installation produced by Aljazeera Contrast, they wrote and directed STILL HERE, a virtual reality experience about the obstacles black women face who re-enter society after being kidnapped and traumatized by the prison industrial complex. It premiered in the New Frontiers section of the Sundance Film Festival. In 2020-2022 they wrote and co-produced on the critically acclaimed cult classic TV series *Betty* (HBO), a coming-of-age story of a diverse group of young women navigating their lives through the predominantly male world of skateboarding. Naima is currently in the metaphorical woods developing several projects in the docu-narrative hybrid space that center people taking back their power after surviving hierarchal abuses internalized by the dominant social order.

Nicole Counts (she/her) is Editorial Director at One World, an imprint of Random House. Books she has worked on have won or been nominated for the National Book Award, the Lambda Literary Award, The Center for Fiction First Novel Prize, various PEN Literary Awards, and more. She is an active member of various publishing equity groups, as well as a long-time volunteer with Well-Read Black Girl. She was a finalist for the 2020 PW Star Watch, an active speaker on publishing/book-related issues, and has been profiled in *Gagosian Quarterly* and *Publishers Weekly*. She has written for *V Magazine, Poets & Writers,*

Brooklyn Magazine, Artnoir, and more.

Paloma Nieto is a Peruvian writer based in Brooklyn. She's an alumna of the Latinx in Publishing Writers Mentorship, the Tin House Summer Workshop, and the Iowa Writers Workshop summer program. Her writing explores love, loss, and migration. She's currently working on her debut novel.

Pilar García Guzmán is a writer from Santiago, Dominican Republic. She is a UIW alum with a BA in English and minors in Creative Writing and Finance. Pilar is now pursuing her MFA in Fiction at Florida Atlantic University, where she serves as Co-Managing Editor of *Swamp Ape Review.* She is working on a novel that explores culture, memory, motherhood, and (you guessed it) grief. Pilar is a self-proclaimed romance novel connoisseur, and she hopes her work makes readers feel as loved and comforted as she does while discovering new work.

Sabrina Shie is a writer from the Bay Area, who is slowly adjusting to life in the desert. She is currently a Program Assistant with Black Mountain Institute in Las Vegas and her work has previously been supported by Napa Valley Writers' Conference and Vermont Studio Center. This is her first publication.

Zabe Bent is a Black, Jamaican New Yorker living between Atlanta and Lisbon. She writes essays, family sagas, and speculative fiction. Zabe works as a city planner and transport engineer, with a focus on safe, sustainable, equitable urban mobility. Her writing has appeared in Breathe FIYAH, the Los Angeles Review of Books, and The Audacity. She currently balances design and policy work with studies toward a PhD, while refining her debut novel.

Cover Art

Scherezade García is a painter, printmaker, and installation artist whose work often explores allegories of history, migration, collective and ancestral memory, and cultural colonization and politics. A cofounder of the Dominican York Proyecto GRÁFICA, she holds an AAS from Altos de Chavón School of Design, a BFA from Parsons School of Design | The New School, and an MFA from The City College of New York, CUNY. García has been featured in solo and duo exhibitions at the Art Museum of the Americas, Clifford Art Gallery at Colgate University, Miller Theater at Columbia University, Lehman College Art Gallery, Crossroads Gallery at the University of Notre Dame, Museo de Arte de Santo Domingo and others. She has participated in the Havana Biennial, the International Biennial of Paintings at Haute de Cagnes, the IV Caribbean Biennial, Trienal Poli/Gráfica de San Juan, Latin American Biennial, BRIC Biennial, Venice Autonomous Biennial, and international fairs. Her work is included in the permanent collections of the Smithsonian American Art Museum, the Art Museum of the Americas, El Museo del Barrio, The Housatonic Museum of Art, El Museo de Arte Moderno in Santo Domingo, and others. Learn more at www.scherezade.net

In the tradition of the Caravans II, from series Agua Firme, 2024
85 x 105 inches (unframed). Acrylic, pigment, charcoal, ink on canvas.

Artist Statement: "I am fascinated with the experience of Las Americas and the crossing of the Atlantic. My work intends to unveil the many ongoing cultural encounters that continuously shape and reshape how we view, perceive, and color America. My work is centered on the politics of inclusion. History plays a central role in my artistic practice of decoding and deconstructing visual narratives of power. I engage history and historical ethnography to pay close attention to traditions, methods, and dominant societal points of view to visually bring forth other voices. Through the deconstruction, the juxtaposition of symbols of constructed Americanness, nationhood and freedom embedded in slavery and oppression, I aim to present the most outrages signs of resistance through the mixing of race, through a fierce optimism. Race, the politics of color (formally and conceptually) is essential to me. The cinnamon figure is a constant in my work since 1996. Mixing all the colors in a palette is an inclusive action, the outcome of such activity is cinnamon color. The new race, represented by my ever-present cinnamon figure states the creation of a new aesthetic This unique aesthetic with new rules originated by the lush landscape, the transplantation, appropriation, and transformation of traditions. Also, the catholic iconography with my mixed-race warrior/angels is my way of colonizing the colonizers...by appropriating, transforming creating new icons. The Atlantic, this blue liquid road and profound obstacle provokes my imagination. The blue sea represents the way out and the frontier. It maps stories about freedom, slavery, and survival, it carries our DNA, and it's an endless source of stories, evolving continuously, reminding us of the fluidity of our identity, our collective memory. Resistance through beauty and joy. Las Americas transformed our world, created new values, a new race, redefined Christianity, and geography. In my neo-baroque tradition, with its inclusivity of spirit, I navigate between tragedy, beauty, carnival, and traces of divinity."

If you enjoyed this issue of *Aster(ix)*
and want to share or see more of our work,
please visit www.asterixjournal.com
or scan the QR code below:

@asterixjournal